These Black Bodies Are . . .
a Blacklandia Anthology

An Inlandia Institute Publication

INLANDIA
INSTITUTE

Editor
Romaine Washington

Assistant Editors
Klarissa Conner, Marcus Muscato

Publications Coordinator
Maria Fernanda Vidaurrazaga

Book Layout & Design
Mark Givens

Cover Art
"Shared Knowledge" by Charles Bibbs ©2023

Printed and bound in the United States
Distributed by Ingram

Published by Inlandia Institute
Riverside, California
www.InlandiaInstitute.org
First Edition

Contents

These Black Bodies Are . . .

Hopeful

Mystical

Mindful

Enlightened

Bodacious

Bearing Witness

Eclectic

Transforming

Introduction

In Ta-Nehisi Coates's book *Between the World and Me*, he proclaims, "In America, it is traditional to destroy the black body – *it is heritage.*" I would definitely agree with this quote based on history and current events. Black bodies were used as machinery to work the plantations and build the mansions of the men referred to as the founding fathers of this country.

Black bodies are threatened at voting polls in the South and endure regular microaggressions as sure as we check our phones and use computers. Black bodies are gunned down while going on a daily jog and listening to music. And after the deaths, Black Bodies rise up to bear witness and demand justice.

These Black Bodies Are . . . snapshots of the human condition in melanated skin and kinky hair. They are not asking permission to wear their kinky hair but rejoicing in the beauty of complexion and natural expression. *These Black Bodies Are* reminding us that though we may sometimes be ethereal and fragile, we are also resilient and determined. We gather strength and are inspired by parents and grandparents. Ms. Opal Lee, grandmother of Juneteenth vowed to use her black body to walk until Juneteenth was recognized as a federal holiday. We remember promises made in the Constitution and even if they were made to our exclusion, we evoke the spirit of the intent so our black bodies and those of our children and children's children have the opportunity to be free. We believe the words of Fanny Lou Hamer "None of us is free until we are all free". These Black Bodies celebrate Juneteenth every day, reminding us that we can, at any age, liberate and empower.

In this book, you will read work where artists speak about post-traumatic slave syndrome, prayers, ghosts, uprisings, reparations, and love, in each selection there is love in its various forms. Two academic papers have been included which I know is highly unusual to have academic writing in a creative collection but the teacher in me could not resist. Both of the papers present commentary that could be the catalyst to encourage discussions on not just the writing but the topics being analyzed. The collection contains work from established and emerging writers, local artists, writers from San Bernardino, and throughout the diaspora.

The collection is divided into eight sections. *These Black Bodies Are* . . . alive and hopeful you will read something that resonates with you. At any given time, our Black bodies are in peril, but we are also 1. hopeful, 2. mindful (mental health), 3. mystical, 4. enlightened (education), 5. bodacious, 6. bearing witness (social justice), 7. eclectic, and 8. transforming. *These Black Bodies Are* inviting you to sit a while and read and we thank you for communing with us.

Romaine Washington
Editor

THESE BLACK BODIES ARE
HOPEFUL

There are always new sounds to imagine;
new feelings to get at.
And always, there is the need
to keep purifying these feelings and sounds
so that we can really see
what we've discovered in its pure state.
So that we can see more and more clearly what we are.
In that way, we can give to those who listen
to the essence, the best of what we are.
- John Coltrane

so my soul may fly: a song

we may use sound.
      each auditory ping
gathered in our arms.
      so much honey
            to smear on the cheek.
                  so many. bells
      that the tongue forgets to.
weep and wander back
and forth like time is.
waiting. a.
set of arms. we may use these
      voices this merging. my
            grandmother's mouth. your
            lap my child. looking up.
      wards. we may.
      use words. though those words
keep saying go.
      back to sleep. where sleep is.
      pieces. of folding back. ears
            to listen to what was. almost dreamed. all this
            and you still. learning to.
            use your name. to sit
                  waiting. in the throat kinked.
                  and curled that. perfect knot that
                        simple tool. refusing to let you
            and soar upwards in fire it   forget how to sing.
      persists like
a wood boat that
drags a long
skirt through
muddy air
      saying this sky is
      mine
            actually
            mine these tiny
                  brown skinned   beings
            that wall this future   all me
      all mine all us   all our time

            ours dancing in a
            belly as the
            body's new brain
the body's hive of hope shifting
                  itself around to dream and do that
                              thing again
how to
      hope
is the way we fly

how to
free a
heart
so it
may
dive.

how to smile on
path towards
glory that for all the
old pain there
weighted
joy like stone.

hope
is a
discipline

NIKIA CHANEY

Make Me[*]

BY NATALIE J. GRAHAM

His hands   make a spire.
I teach   the word   steeple.

    We dream at God.
I say,   *God, be close to us.*
He says,   *if God can't*
make me   *a bird,*
    who can?

   His heart, a ripe peach, his wild boy-song, jubilant fire.

                        When I say,
                        I can't breathe,
                        I mean,
                        I am afraid.

No window in this corner of night
   no hopeful crows calling for the dawn,
      no nesting with their babies under pine,
         no nudging them into air.
                 See the dark yawn spread,
                 the gloom-blotched murk,
                 night, a giant lily's bloom
                 unfurling a fan of shadows.

When I say matter,   when I say lives,   I mean,
     marvel   at the pinnacle

his brown hands make,

his brown face
    rising,
        draped   in   ginger   lamplight.

---

*   This poem refers to "The Corner of Night and Morning" by Amy Lowell

Alternate Ending

after Safia Elhillo

BY KENNY CARROLL

The boy opens his eyes
and watches the bullet hover before him
Its metal cadaver still spinning
He blinks again
and there are two
He closes his eyes and finds a song
somewhere inside the gunshots
It seems like a sort of forever
but the alive kind
The next time he opens his eyes
he sees an empty clip
And he exhales
And the officer drops his gun
And the boy hugs his mother
And the only thing left hollow on the street
is the empty shells
:::
Everywhere the bullets
stop working
Some kind of
magic
Some kind of
God
No one agrees

but no one has to
Everybody is alive
Every table full
In every way
Another war
ends
No more bullets
They try to get creative
but the grenades don't explode
The knives can only
chop bread
Nothing is killing the way it's supposed to
and none of the killers can kill
:::
I wouldn't call it a better world
just different
I wouldn't call it peace
just a quiet place to start

Unbound

BY SHARON M. WILLIAMS

Are they camel-colored vertical blinds left open for the sun, or

a fence of weathered, splintered wood juxtaposed against
the neighbor's moss-colored grass and grinds of bedroom sounds
too harsh to be melodies?

Are they thriving snake plants who keep overgrowing their pots, or

people of color trying to kick out a cement ceiling
until their toes fold back into themselves crippling their feet
binding roots no one can see until they're repotted
in a casket?

Are they swirling clouds of white, blue, and gray colors in the sky, or

a chain gang of round bottoms viewed from privatized prison cells
where they incarcerate and harvest our young
for their bodies?

Are they a vibrant spectrum of birds flying freely over rooftops, or

rainbow-colored children with their arms stretched out
trying to use bandanas and t-shirts for capes
as they run...in cages?

Are they land snails after a storm with seemingly nowhere to go, or

are they voices planted in fertilized fields of schools,
churches, and park benches, standing on corners, lining parades,
speaking at the family dinner table, speaking—speaking—speaking
their truth?

uncuffed, uncaged, unpotted

Unbound

Melanin Canyon

BY MITCHELL WASHINGTON

They wonder why the road curves the way it does
Swaying bodies, splitting eye gazes for small gasps of breath
I feel the ebb and flow on these corners
Walls that rush up on you then disappear into the distance

Blue slivers of love down here
Softly touching my peripheral.
A breeze reveals chocolate cliffs
Ravens fly, floating like a desert sky
I sunbathe, All Day
Just to look up and feel at home . . .
Thin beige bushes paint the water green
Beyond Serene

Wishes whispering in the wind sing hypnotic hymns
"Swallow me whole sweet canyon,
UV rays transform into melanin"
Rock falls create drum solos and a mist of dust
I find myself squinting a lot here.
Maybe because my peanut size brain
Can't handle
So much beauty at once

A Brooklyn Saturday Walk
Circa 2022 (4/16/22)

BY SHONDA BUCHANAN

My daughter is perfectly pregnant.
We inch our way down Eastern Parkway.

Her nearly three-year-old son runs ahead
as fast as his caterpillar legs can go.

A bullhorn cracks. Ten brothers all donned in purple jerseys
shout Black history truths at onlookers. Wake up. It's time.

African hawkers sell shirts, shades, shoes, purses,
socks, jewelry, shea butter, whatever the people in Crown Heights need.

Day writhes with too much cologne against
sour smell of fish wafting out of Asian market

under scent of jerk sauce on charred chicken. Fire sirens harangue the day.
We hit the park. Children scream, crisscrossing the playground frantically.

Remembering how to play. Trying to outrace the last two years.
My daughter closes her eyes and smiles.

We are in walking labor. We are here.
Life in our teeth. Life happening still. I snap our selfie.

Don't post that picture, she says with a deadly Taurus smile.
I won't. But she can't make me not write a poem

about this moment. How passers-by bless her, laugh into our space.
Covet her buttery globed belly.

How my second grandson swims inside her, far too comfortable.
Five days late. How my toddler grandson thinks he's flying when he runs.

Maybe he is. Maybe we are. I have to write a poem, I think.
I have to hold this moment of bald gazes

atop city grit, laced with spring sun. With hope.
We are beautiful in our mother-daughter dance.

My child having a baby who will be her child. A second son.
My daughter. She is as perfect as the Cairo moon.

Beauty of Community

BY VICKI LEE

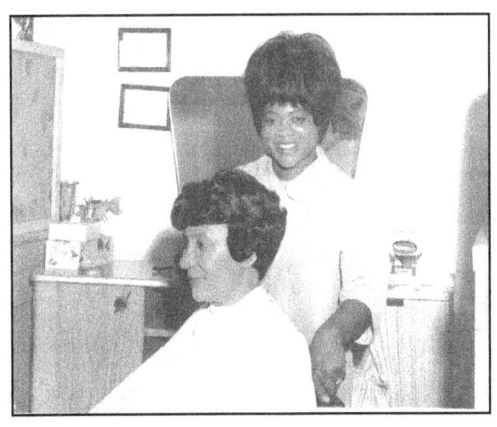

Some people called Lee's House of Beauty the transformation salon. You would walk in torn up from the floor up and leave fried, dyed, and finger waved to the side. My mom, Naomi was most famous for her finger waves! Mom had a boom box at the front of the salon. As soon as you entered you would hear gospel, blues, or jazz to welcome you in. She enjoyed cooking and you could often smell the aroma of fried chicken and sweet potato pie from outside the beauty shop door. My father knew how important it was for my mother to cook and share it with her customers in the community. He would make sure to buy extra groceries to make that happen. Sometimes he would even cook collard greens. Boy, could he cook collard greens! Between the food, getting shampooed, relaxed, and having good conversations, my mom's salon was a home away from home for her clients.

The shop was an extension of home for me too. It was as much a symbol of the love between my mother and father as I was. My mom loved styling hair so much that she would fix strangers' hair for free. When she told Golden (that is really my father's name – which also describes him as a person) that she wanted to be a beautician he worked to put her through school and when she said she wanted her own salon, he worked three jobs to make it happen. The only requirement my mom had was for the beauty shop to be financially self-sufficient. He loved her so much, he wanted to make sure that she was able to do something fulfilling that brought her joy and in return, she gave all that she had to share joy and kindness with everyone else.

I remember that one of the families in the neighborhood did not have enough food to last through the month. My mom told my father; he went grocery shopping and purchased food for that family. He told the family that there was a big sale at the grocery store, and they wanted to share the food with others. After that, my mom started cooking and taking food to the beautyshop.

With many hairstyles, it would take two to three hours from start to finish; during that time clients would talk with Mom. People shared their victories and problems with her. She would listen and pray with them in the shampoo room. If my mom was aware of a financial need that one of her clients had she would either take care of it herself or find someone who could. Her clients became extended family, and I grew up feeling like I was related to everyone in San Bernardino.

While it was great to have an ever-expanding family there were also times of sorrow when a customer would die. It was literally like losing a family member. Mom would insist on doing their hair and make-up at the mortuary because she knew exactly how they wanted it to be done. Although it was sad, I always took her and worked with her until she was satisfied with the final look.

My mother was a community mother in so many ways but she also knew how to have fun. She loved entertaining and telling jokes and she was quite the singer, gospel, and blues mainly. Occasionally, we would have little talent shows full of hugs, applause, and laughter. Mom knew how to change the mood of the shop according to who was there.

At the time I didn't see it as much as a point of pride but more of irritation. I began working as a bookkeeper in the shop and I saw my mom and dad help out people all the time. Teens being teens, one day

I told my mom that she would be a millionaire if she didn't give away so much money. Sometimes people would write checks on insufficient funds which infuriated me because Naomi would give away free services whenever someone needed them. I felt like they took her for granted and saw her kindness as a weakness.

She was always giving and putting everyone else's needs in front of her. Maybe it is a generational thing, but I told myself I was going to make sure that I would never be like her. I would make sure that my needs were met first and there would be a balance of how much of myself I would give away. I was going to take care of myself and make sure I rested. I was only going to do or give if I wanted to and the word "no" would be my default.

I felt that everyone was pulling on my mother's hem to clean, cook, fix hair, mend clothes, pay someone else's bills, and listen and listen and listen to problems, around the clock. My mother gave beyond what I thought any reasonable person should; I thought all this sacrifice was not healthy nor required to be a good person. I vowed that I would never be like her.

Now that I am older and wiser, I understand that when you attempt to make a difference by helping others, you have to do what God has put on your heart to do. If people are taking advantage of your kindness, that is between them and their God. As Christians, when possible, we are to help those in need. We must let God determine if they are need or in greed.

Wife-Mother-Sister-Friend-Beautician-Entrepreneur-Prayer Warrior-Entertainer. Naomi owned Lee's House of Beauty and birthed and nurtured a community in which she was the heart. Decades have come and gone; I still feel like I am related to many of the people in San Bernardino. Naomi and Golden are no longer alive but each morning I wake up I ask myself whom can I help today, what can I give, and how can I make a difference.

Sistah-hood Sojourns

BY SHEILA MARCHBANKS

Remarkable being among the fire and brilliance of others
　　Can radiate flames to warm and comfort our waning embers.

Astounding how the harmony of joyful voices
　　Can balm the breaks in our hearts.

Miraculous the gifts that are unknowingly given
　　Can be a meeting of minds, souls, and spirits.

Triumphant yet tired, walking hand in hand in love, in hope, in faith,
　　And most importantly in sync with God, our Creator. . .

Experiencing all that we do, He knew that we needed the ties that
Help us to hold and to carry on. As we live out this glorious gift of life
Overflowing with blessings, yet not devoid of burdens, thankful and
Grateful we stay buoyed by the strong, bountiful, and blazingly
Beautiful bonds of sisterhood.

Church Mothers

by Thomasina Sanders

the first "praise the lord!"
woke me slowly,
easing me back into the wooden pew.
my surroundings sounding
suddenly larger than hand claps
mimicking volcanic laughter.

another "praise the lord!"
was let loose
to climb stained glass windows,
hang itself on the blue illuminated cross,
affixed directly above a podium;
where words were offered
as grains of uncooked rice.

in every direction
people stood.
i joined them
unfolding my comfort
to mingle with others

and amid this routine jubilee,
rounded shoulders,
cloaked quietly beneath
a hand-knitted shawl,
moved lethargically
in front of the mass and
began speaking –

offering honor to god

his servants
dependents
and anyone else
within the sound of her time-stained voice

as she spoke of her thankfulness
for being able "to get up this morning"
and "worship in the house of the lord"
instead of being bed-ridden
like the weeks before--

the choir slowed its praises.
hummed quietly in harmony
playing her personal soundtrack
to every ailment she defeated
under the blanket of
"his good graces"
of which she will never be worthy.

she said "thank you"
in three different pitches repeatedly
until others joined in her appreciation

as she wept,
lamenting "thank you Jesus"
her legs moved her body
stubbornly along the first row

back to her personal seat
back to her private meditation
back to her space

were she was
commonly known as
Mother

Our Garden

by Maya Adenihun

Our ancestors
were as prosperous
as endless gardens
of fruits and roses.
Savoring
as love drips from their mouths
intaking the scent of bliss
as it infuses.
But such paradise was stolen
by weeds of ignorance
and brutality.
We were ripped
and replanted;
pushed into the ground
to lick dirt
until we were shoved into Hell.
Instead of souls,
there were screams,
instead of pulsing
there was ache,
and angels
were dangling
instead of flying.
Yet even
in such inhumane realities,
we are able

to pull ourselves out.
It is not an easy task
to rip each other out of dirt
nor is it pretty.
But we inherit strength.
Strength to use our oozing blood
to paint roses
into our own
creations and future.
Yet roses can not flourish
if they are ripped open
by anxious, guilty hands.
They grow best with care,
commitment, and belief.
They will not become perfect
but beautiful
out of our love and labor.
We stretch our hands
out of the ground
we were planted in
and grow with joy
in the sun.
No matter where we are
we join together
and thrive.
We have become again
what we were stolen from.

MAYA ADENIHUN

The Essence of My Blackness

by Deborah Tarver Waters

The essence of my blackness
spreads across the sky
riding the beauty of His soul
spreading my joy power and love
in Him

The essence of my blackness
rejoices in His presence
spreading throughout the world
riding high the knowledge
that God loves me
more than anything known

The essence of my blackness
escapes any attempt
to hold me back
from changing the hate
of those who jealously guard
their biased power of racism
polluting the world
with limited knowledge
that I am who I am
a child of the living God
and since He's for me
their attempt
of pulling me down
keeping me down
are childish

as my blackness
the sweetness of
my blackness
conquers them

The essence of my blackness
rolls like thunder across skies
electrifying clouds with tears
that wash away any fears
of oppression
winds turning in the right direction
my rights I win
because greater
am I when I am in Him

The essence of my blackness
enables me to conquer
racist rants
of a world that would throw me down
rising on wings of angels
powered by love divine
a sign that since He's for me
I am unconquerable
because the essence of my blackness
explodes into greatness
and I rise on the wind
of His Spirit

The essence of my blackness
holds me folds me molds me
into His image
and I imagine

that I really can do
all things
through Christ
who strengthens me
The essence of my blackness
embraces the secrets
of His soul

In Celebration

after Lucille Clifton

BY SHIRLEY JONES-LUKE

I'm here to celebrate
your version of living.
You are my model
Babylon's blessing.
Black & female
I only saw what you allowed
me to see. Was it you?
I cross the bridge
made of star shine & clay,
My hand holding your hand.
I am here to celebrate
with you always.
I saw what tried to kill you
because it tried to kill me.

At The End of A Long Day

by George Hammons

for Joshua

I walk past my son's room
only to see that he has folded his hands
and knelt next to his bed to pray
I am a bit startled
My son talks to God

I stand for just a moment
searching for something wise to say
but to interrupt his prayer would seem wrong
after all, I gave up such godly conversations
for what now seems to have been, so long
So, I say nothing and instead move on

Asking myself
for what do eleven-year-old Black boys pray
I suppose that perhaps a difficult math test, or a schoolyard conflict
may lay in wait for the following day
I note that he did not come to me
and has instead
invested his plea
with someone over my head

But I return for just a moment and peek
into his doorway
looking in at where he now quietly lay
and I ask myself (again)
"For what do eleven-year-old black boys *pray*?"

Psalm 71:14

BY XCLUSIVELYTAYLOR

You Will Not Die Here

by Shonda Buchanan

for Andrew Johnson, my unborn grandson,
and my first grandson, Angelo Lewis

Dear beautiful black wrestler boy
you are not the cutting of your locs.

You are instead the lotus wind that escapes from slits in the laughing earth
when a great tale is being told, when fault lines shift,
when virgins disappear when houses crumble to dust.

You are not the scissor-hands of someone you trusted
yanking out your roots and branches.

You are instead Hannibal's 37 elephants, 15,000 horses, 30,000
soldiers making the Alps tremble in a destined march to end
an empire of tired, corrupt men.

You are not the timber sound of your hair falling
on a wrestling mat.

You are instead the tender moment when language
convinces love to come, to trust
and live in a dangerous place anyway.

You are not decent, complicit eyes ignoring your public rape.
Not one man's small useless organ beating in placid,
soon-to-die chest.
You are not the weakness of your knees,
Not the tightness of your throat. Not the doubt cracking your lungs.
  Your back to us, your cheeks dry,

shocked by the sudden taste of history in your mouth.
Boy becoming man
Man becoming leader
Leader becoming king.

Returned to us.

You are every black child, black student,
black boy, man, father, husband, uncle, cousin
they tried to keep down.
You are the porcelain of dreams, the wet of water
the cold jade of fire on the tip of a poet's spear.
You are the darkest of darkness
where beautiful black magic is born.
You are magic.
You are gris-gris and Coptic crosses.

You are a Black life that matters.
You are not defeated.
You are the precious spell I cast when I write.
Your body is an ancient tongue that holds babies'
placenta-palm secrets.
You are Wanda Coleman's ghost, pissed and on fire.
You are the ancestors singing of you
long before the stars wept slave blood when America was born.
You are the blade we polished again and again
by antebellum fire's light
so we could live. So we could get you here.

You will not die with their hands in your hair.
We will not die with their hands in our hair.

You are James Baldwin's caterpillar hatchet eyes.
You are family reunions and first loves and teeth under pillows.

You are books and prayer beads in the hands of children.
You are Aretha's two changes of outfits in her casket.
You are cowrie shells in the hands of elders.

You are a beautiful blackrose boy
in a field of beautiful blackrose boys.

You are alive.
You are magic.
You are alive.
You are magic.
You, we, will never be defeated.
You are alive. You are magic.
Beautiful black wrestler boy.
Black doctor girl. Black communications, English, Ethnic studies, an-
thropology, sociology major. Black filmmaker. Black politician in the
making. Black college president. Black parents. Black coder. Black chef.
Black rapper. Black musician. Black journalist. Black photographer.
Black administrator. Black opera singer. Black businessman, woman,
Black student.
Black child.
You are magic. You are magic.
Magic.

my vena cava

by NOMAD the Poet

you've carried me out of the trenches of Death,
my heartbeat is strong

you've led me through unknown lands
where fear transformed
into prosperity,
my heartbeat is strong

you've strengthened Our chambers —
weaving tapestries of creation
and resilience
from hate and confusion.
my heartbeat is strong with

each beat— a prophecy,
predicated on my Ancestors' tombs.
each beat— a new legacy,
bred from my Ancestors' wounds.

my blood made into wine
with each defiant fist, they held high,
a revolution not televised,
but organized in church rooms.

my heartbeat is strong.

Hope Fool

BY STEPHANI MAARI BOOKER

"...The endgame is always going to be death, so how
hopeful can anyone be?"
—Terrance Hayes

Like saying hope is only for immortals,
or just for the children too young to know
what mortality is, for the imaginary
or the innocent — the ignorant. For fools.
The afterlife simply desperate delusion,
a denial of the brevity of breath.
We're all fools? All believers are bumpkins?
All aspirations are asinine?
"Where's life, there's hope" — a cliché. No life, no hope
— an axiom. Paradise imagines the hope
in no hope. We imagination makers who dream
against death? Yes, we will dream ourselves immortal.
No hope, no life. No life in being wise.
Be fools. Believe we can live forever. Be alive.

Note: The epigraph is from an interview with poet Terrance Hayes done by
Hanif Abdurraqib in "My Past and Future Assassin," the cover story of
Poets & Writers magazine, July/August 2018, page 32.

THESE BLACK BODIES ARE
MYSTICAL

a handful of earth - a handful of sky
Octavia Butler

Flightsong

by Elizabeth Gibbs

*They say the people could fly. Say that long ago in Africa, some
of the people knew magic. And they would walk up on the air
like climbin' up on a gate. And they flew like blackbirds over
the fields. Black, shiny wings flappin against the blue up there.*
- The People Could Fly, by Virginia Hamilton

Shackles bit into my wrists and ankles. Chains rattled. My head hurt. I pushed against the pain, trying to remember how I came to be here, wherever here is. I remember being grabbed from behind and hit. I remember watching my legs crumble beneath me as I fell. I remember hearing loud voices and words I did not understand. I remember those things but nothing more.

I woke up in a dark space crowded with men, women, and children. Many were weeping. I asked everyone around me the same question: "Do you know me?" Most did not speak my language and those who did could tell me nothing.

Days later, strange white men packed us front to back on long, hard bunks in a great ship. Howls of anguish and the stench of death kept us company on a long, strange journey. Many gods were called: Oludumare, Esu, Oya, Shango, Obatala, Yemanja, and more. Since I did not know which might be mine, I prayed to all of them for deliverance. My prayers went unanswered, and I was left grieving for a family, a name, and a life I no longer remembered. My soul was gone.

We reached a land called Virginia in the spring and were shoved onto wooden platforms. There we were pushed, prodded, poked, and sold off like cattle. My body was strong in spite of the harsh treatment I endured. A white man calling himself Jeremiah Scott bought me. He told me my name would be Nathaniel. He took me to a place called Twin Oaks and put me to work in his tobacco fields.

Hard work was no stranger to my body, and it did all that was asked of it. Slavery in this strange land was bad enough, but not knowing who I was made it worse, for I had no past to look back on and no future to look forward to. I was caught in an empty and rootless today. I often wished for death. Even so, something woke me every morning and placed one foot in front of the other. Something kept my hands reaching for food and water. Something raised my eyes to the sun's passage in the day and the stars' presence at night. Over time I learned to shut down the longings, the despair, the loss, and the anger. I did what was asked of me quietly and efficiently, one of Massa Scott's 'good' slaves.

Occasionally an odor or sound would tug at the edge of familiarity to awaken shrouded flashes of remembrance, but I could not hold onto them. Then the reality of my life would threaten to crush me with its weight. To push the pain away I ran alone at night in the woods that border the plantation. The sound of my bare feet pounding the earth over and over dulled the heartache and the rhythm of muscles pumping under my skin, help to lift the burden from my heart even as I wished I could pound and pump hard enough to soar to freedom in the heavens. The feelings lasted only as long as my strength. When that gave out, I collapsed and gasped the rest of my anguish into the earth. The other slaves sensed the dark cloud over my head and left me to myself. I was alone until Sarah came.

She was like a little sister to me, kind, caring, and compassionate. We often found ourselves planting tobacco side by side under the watchful eyes of the overseer. Our wordless contests to see who could plant their way to the end of a row before the other was broken only by secret glances and quick grins. As fast as I planted, Sarah was always faster, and she always finished first.

She was first in almost everything else too, especially daring and dangerous things. Many slaves at Twin Oaks talk about running, but Sarah was the first to do it. All those stories around the campfire about Harriet Tubman running slaves north on the Underground Railroad and never losing a passenger went straight to her head. She would tell me how she'd lie awake in bed, night after night, straining to hear the sounds of Harriet's voice singing out Swing low, sweet chariot, the signal to go.

Harriet never did come to Twin Oaks, so Sarah up and left on her own. She got as far as the river before they caught her. They dragged her back, strung her up by her wrists between two posts, and made us all watch while they put the lash to her. She took that whipping better than most men could. Never made a sound, just pressed her full lips into a thin tight line and spit rocks with her eyes.

The fever hit after the beating, and she was sick for a long time. I was sick to think she might die, but she didn't. Sarah got better because Juba, the local midwife and herb woman Massa Scott called in. After he saw how she fixed Sarah, he gave her a cabin in the quarter and paid her to care for the rest of us.

Juba was free, tall, gnarled, and ageless like a baobab tree. The first time I saw her was at Sarah's cabin. I looked in the window one evening, hoping to find Sarah awake. She wasn't but Juba was burning some foul-smelling leaves in the fireplace and fanning the curling gray-white smoke into the room. She stopped suddenly, turned toward the window, and saw me. She froze, looking for all the world like one of Massa Scott's scarecrows, stiff, quiet, and still as death. She didn't say a thing. She stared straight into my head like she'd seen a ghost. I backed off straight away and high-tailed it to my cabin.

Folk on the plantation said Juba knew juju and that she didn't come here on the white man's ship as we did. They said she came on the wind and is working her way from plantation to plantation looking for someone.

Most folks kept shy of Juba, and I did too after I caught her looking at me in strange ways every time our paths crossed. Her eyes screamed at me as she swept past, but she never spoke a word.

It became easier not to think about Juba's strange behavior when my feelings for Sarah began to change. All of a sudden, the curve of her neck and shoulder fascinated me, the sound of her voice lifted me out of my misery, and seeing her smile became more important to me than eating or sleeping. I savored every minute with her, remembered every detail of every minute, and savored it all over again when I was alone.

It was amazing to me that I could feel such pleasure; that another person could make such a deep change in how I felt about life. I was actually happy, but I shut that feeling down like I shut down all the others and kept silent because a relationship between us was forbidden. Sarah was of breeding age and would soon be matched with an older slave who had a proven record of siring children. Their children would be sold off to feed the growing demands of Virginia's slave market and fatten the coffers at Twin Oaks. My silence lasted one long, bittersweet year.

It was Sarah who ended it. One summer night under the big chestnut tree in the back fields, she told me she cared for me, and she wanted us to be together no matter what might happen. We became lovers then. The happiness of that time seeped through my skin like honey to sweeten my heart, but fear tied my gut into knots. If Massa Scott found out about us I would be sold south, he would breed Sarah and I would lose her forever. Our situation was hopeless.

By winter Sarah was restless and moody. My heart sank because I sensed what was coming. Freedom is what she craved, and freedom was her solution to our plight. She begged me to run with her. Said she'd go by herself if she had to.

I had no love for slavery but going north seemed impossible. The night patrols had increased. All slave gatherings were closely watched. "Besides," I'd tell her, "No one who ran ever came back to tell us what freedom felt like or how to go north to find it."

That's what I said to her, but truthfully, I felt like the fox at the end of a hunt, cornered and afraid. She was right. Going north was the only way for us to be together, but I have never been off the plantation, so how could I hope to get us safely to some whispered-about mythical destination like north?

Jeremiah Scott made sure that we all knew the punishment for running; public whipping, branding, cutting off a leg or foot, or being sold. Sale would part us swiftly and forever. I was unwilling to change it or to watch the expression on her face if we tried and failed. It would be more than I could bear. Sarah was my link to life. So, I made the decision to stall her as long as possible, treasure the time we had left and not think any more about a future I couldn't shape. I preferred her anger.

That I got. It battered down my thin wall of happiness and fed the frustration of my inability to protect the woman I loved. I felt weighed down by despair and accepted what I knew to be the calm before the storm.

The storm broke the day Sarah told me she carried my child in her belly. She said she would wait no longer for me to make up my mind. She planned to run soon with or without me. Said she'd rather die and take the child with her than birth it in bondage. The joy I felt in hearing that I would be a father was overshadowed by fear. I knew I could lose everything that mattered to me if I didn't put the fear aside and run north in spite of the danger.

That night the devil and his demons rode my dreams so hard I couldn't sleep. I sought relief in the stillness and solitude of the forest bordering the slave quarter. I knew I had to run with Sarah. I could not let her go alone. To go and fail would be unbearable, but to let her go alone was unthinkable. Running would outdistance my demons for a little while.

I raced down a heavily wooded trail. Suddenly a song filled with pain and longing broke the stillness. It stirred my blood, tugged at my mind, and stopped me dead in my tracks. It came from the stand of hemlocks to my left. My bare feet padded quietly over uneven ground to the edge of the clearing. I peeked around a tree to see Juba, arms outstretched, head back and eyes closed, hovering about four hand spans in the air! The sound was coming from her! I gasped and froze. Startled, she opened her eyes, floated across the clearing, and dropped to the ground in front of me. She motioned for silence with a finger to her lips and whispered, "Ajuba, Nathaniel. Aye l'oja, orun n'ile."

In a flash, the meaning of those words rose from the foggy depths of my mind, "The world is a marketplace; heaven is our home." She spoke my language! My mind went wild with hows and whys, but all I could do was utter the one thing I repeated over and over to others before being loaded onto the ship that brought me here. "Do you know me?"

"Yes, I know you." Her voice was gentle. "Problem is, you don't know me." She knew me! Juba knew me! Someone knew me! Tears welled in my eyes. Questions flooded my mind and poured from my mouth. Hope and joy, mixed with confusion. If she knew me, why hadn't she said so before now and how in heaven's name could she fly?

She said she couldn't call my life back or tell me her secrets. "The remembering must come from inside you, Nathaniel. It's all there. Locked inside. I recognized you straight off and my heart nearly burst clean out my chest until I realized the slavers stole your soul and left you empty as a pig trough after feeding time."

Crushed, I sank to the ground. Juba joined me and we sat in silence. Suddenly, in spite of being cold and tired, I grabbed a thought that flashed by. If Juba could fly maybe there was a way she could fly Sarah and me north to freedom.

I asked but it was not to be. Juba said, "I know you and Sarah must leave soon, but I cannot fly you to freedom. I am the only one with the power of flightsong. I cannot carry both of you. You must leave on foot, but I can help you when you are ready."

She said we would go to a place called Canada. The passage of the Fugitive Slave Act allowed slavers to enter free states and capture runaways. Canada was the only place of safety. Juba, had been helping the abolitionists run slaves north for the past few years, but now the overseers were casting suspicious looks in her direction, and free or not, she suspected her usefulness might be coming to an end.

We set our escape for the night of spring jamboree. White and Black folk alike would be eating, singing, dancing, and swapping stories at the big house and in the quarter. When the time came, Sarah and I sat in Juba's cabin. She took a stick and drew a map on the dirt floor. She sketched a group of stars called the Little Chariot.

The last star in the hitching arm was the North Star. We were to keep it on our left as we made our way through the forest at the edge of the plantation. She told us to follow an old Manahoac Indian trail along the Rappahannock River until we reached a large farm. There would be a quilt hung over the front gate. There, a Quaker by the name of Ripley would hide us in his barn until we could be passed from station to station on the Underground Railroad north to Philadelphia and from there to Canada.

I begged Juba to leave with us. I was terrified to be away from the one person who knew my life. Juba said she'd be missed if she didn't make her rounds of the sick before sun up. Said she'd catch up with us in Philadelphia and go with us from there to Canada. We went over Juba's sketch again and again until we were sure of every detail. Juba wiped the earth clean with a bare foot and bid us farewell.

Everything was as Juba said. With the North Star as our guide, we reveled in the sensation of freedom, of being able to eat, sleep, talk, or do nothing as we wished. Late one evening, about one day's travel from the river, I woke up when Sarah turned over in my arms. I kissed her forehead. She smiled as her brown eyes opened. She sat up, stretched her arms to the sky, took a small cloth from her pocket, and spread it on the ground. Her hands plunged into one of our sacks and brought out two large hunks of cornbread and some smoked fish, which we ate hungrily.

We were washing our meal down with water from the calabash when we heard a swooshing sound, followed by the crunch of leaves and twigs. Startled, we looked back in the direction of the trail to see Juba coming toward us at a run, waving her arms and shouting, "Come, children, up! No time to waste! I'se been found out! Massa Scott and his slave catchers are on my trail. Can't wait no longer; have to leave here like I came and take you two with me!"

Sarah put her hands protectively over her belly. "But how will we outrun the slavers?"

Juba sighed and looked to the heavens past the place where the North Star had begun to glow. She looked to Sarah and to me and said, "We gon' fly!"

Sarah's mouth dropped open in amazement. What she said next made my knees buckle.

"Yep, we gon' fly if Nathaniel can help."

Juba told Sarah to watch the path and come get us if Scott and his men showed up. Then she marched me through the poplar trees toward three large rocks. Once seated behind them and out of Sarah's sight, Juba took my hands in hers, and with kindness and love in her voice said, "Nathaniel, I didn't want to do this now, but we don't have a choice. You must remember or we are lost."

Juba untied her shoulder sack, pulled out a small leather pouch, took a pinch of the yellow powder, held my jaw with one hand, and put the powder under my tongue with the other. She sat back, locked her eyes on my bewildered ones, and said, "Nathaniel, I know you are afraid. I understand but now you must move past your fear." Then she began to chant. Over and over, she repeated phrases in our language. I stared into her eyes and let their deep pools of compassion draw me in. I let the words and their meaning soothe me: Remember, Nathaniel, Remember, the earth is a marketplace. Heaven is our home.

Soon my silent tears were replaced by sobs as years of sorrow and loss fell out of my body. When I thought surely, I was drained dry, she began to push my shoulders with her hands and repeated over and over; "Akinyele Doumbiya, wake up! Asai, Baru Doumbiya, dibi koro! Wake up!"

Her words rang in my ears. The yellow powder seared my throat. A sound vibrating deep within burned away the fog around my soul. Time slowed. Fear and confusion dissolved. The sound swelled, throbbed, and hummed. I was not prepared for its power of it. A great bubble welled up and exploded in my throat. A howl roared out of my mouth. My frozen spirit shattered like glass. The shards fell back into the past, leaving me suddenly and curiously empty. Juba's voice filled that emptiness. "Akinyele Doumbiya, dibi koro. Wake up! Wake up!"

Recognition rushed into the open wound of my soul and made a home. I shouted with joy. I was Akinyele Doumbiya! This was my name! Juba was calling my name! Cleansed by the release and buoyed by my naming, I was filled with a sense of wonder and power.

"Juba! Grandmother! I remember." Pieces of my lost life flashed before me; the village compound where I was born, the faces of my parents, my brothers, and sisters. I saw the river, the forests, and the majesty of Mt Joro, home of the Ancestors, in the distance.

One powerful image stood strong and clear above the rest. The knowledge of flightsong ran in my blood as it ran in my grandmother's. I had been traveling to the gathering of elders to complete my initiation into manhood when I was kidnapped on the War Road two days out from the village.

My song trumpeted through my veins. I opened my mouth to let it out. Juba began to sing too and we smiled at each other in perfect harmony as we rose together into the night.

The sound of horses' hooves, running feet, and loud voices shattered our moment of joy. We descended as Sarah appeared, chest heaving.

"Juba! Nathaniel! Massa Scott! Massa Scott!" She threw herself into my arms.

The memory of what happened next will be with me forever. Three of the slavers rushed in. Juba's hand dipped into her sack and emerged with a knife. She plunged it into the chest of the red-haired overseer who reached for Sarah. He roared with pain, stumbled and fell. A volley of shots rang out. I watched in horror as Juba crumbled to the ground, a gaping wound in her chest. I watched her body release her life's blood, her soul and my link to family and home.

Red-hot with anger I sunk my fist into soft white flesh. I did not feel my legs carry me forward, but I did feel them crumble under blows landing on my head and body as. I passed out.

When I came to I found myself cradled in Sarah's lap looking up into the face of Jeremiah Scott, Master of Twin Oaks.

"Nigger, it's the auction block for you." He looked at Sarah whose swollen belly was no longer hidden by wide skirts and aprons. He laughed and slapped his riding crop against his thigh.

"Well," he boomed, bending over to look into her still-defiant eyes. "Your whelp should bring a good price. It's the only thing saving you from whipping, and branding gal."

He pointed to Juba's body. Tears of grief rose behind my eyes, but anger would not let them fall. I longed to feel my hands around his throat. He turned to his men. "I'll take Red back to see the doc. Bury the old bitch. Chain these two up. I'll be back in the morning with a wagon to haul'em home."

Home to them but the end of everything, absolutely everything for us. I lost my grandmother. Sarah and I will lose our freedom before we can claim it. We'll lose our child and each other. I saw no way out. Without Juba my flight song is useless.

Exhausted after our struggle, we fell asleep. I woke up a short time later to a high thrumming sound was making a flightsong. She woke up then, her eyes wide and blinking. Her mouth formed a surprised "Oh."

"Hush," I told her, suddenly understanding what was happening. "It is our miracle." The sounds thrummed louder. "But how? How?" she asked, astounded that the sounds were coming from her.

"Sarah, it's how Juba would have gotten us over the river. She needed me to remember who I am so I could make flightsong. The magic is passed down in the blood. Our child carries it in his blood, as I carry it in mine!" I joined my flightsong to the baby's. The flightsong well widened and warmed. We struggled against our bonds to stand. The guards moved toward us, guns at the ready.

"The chains, Nathaniel, the chains!" whispered, Sarah. The well of flightsong spread. The chains snapped. We heard gunshots. Bullets bounced off the womb of sound surrounding us. Scott's men stood dumbfounded. Sarah's belly quieted. The air around us throbbed and hummed. There was a pleasant buzzing feeling, and we were enfolded in something warm and soft without weight or color. The air began to vibrate with a ripeness I could almost taste.

"I put my arm around Sarah as I stepped up on the air carrying her with me. We rose slowly and steadily, higher and higher, over the treetops, off to the river and whatever lay beyond. It was a wonder. The sun's light washed the land laid out before us. Trees, fields, and farms swam past. The sensation of flying wrapped its comforting familiarity around me. How quickly memories emerged now that the door to my past had swung open.

The Rappahannock River looked mighty like the river Jordan to me; wide, swift, and welcoming. Brown water, powerful and strong, forging its own way as it travels from source to sea; a force at home with itself. I felt like the river then, my source is known at last, the sea of my destiny far off but certain.

I feel that way now when I watch Sarah with our children, William Ajani and Juba Asabi. The feeling deepens whenever I remember that it was Juba, my grandmother, and Sarah, my wife, whose love and strength helped me regain what had been stolen: my freedom, my memory, and the most important home I could ever know – my soul – myself.

In the Meadow

BY JENNIFER MARITZA McCAULEY

Dear Mami,
Let's go to the meadow
Let's start anew
Amid wind-nudged reeds
And flapping floras
Let's gobble up the smear
Of sky, let's run to the lake
And swim in its wrinkled
Blue face

Let's call to the catbirds
Our voices heaving and wild
Let's sing to the drifting doe
Let's love the jumping cardinal

Let's run to the oaken cabin
It's small and perfect for love
Let's live anew in that place,
You'll cook sometimes, I will too

We'll trade secrets in wooden walls
You'll smile often, I will too.

Dear Mami,
Let's go to the meadow
Let's finally exhale

Survive

BY ERIC DEVAUGHNN

If I am to do more than just survive, let clouds first part in their
praise
Let rains cleanse the gutters running with the blood spilled in protest

If I am to survive beyond what she expects of any of us, let the earth
first applaud
and trees overgrow the concrete streets on which knees have knelt
necks into nothingness
Let rivers carve a new path through wall street and wash away the
stink of exchange
Call the wind to push through capitols and let the breeze be our only
state

And announce that I am here.

Untitled

by Harry Palacio

Peridot in heather; obols loosened from manacles as though blind
    eyes of mauve-

Finery which was crow-wolf, parsnip and Indian beadwork where a
    coven of azure hung

A testament in dearth upended the quiet; a brow hung like stone
    wagwom that fastened a thread-

like gut of stars-

Regal in every right, the chiding of indigenous drums a bedlam, a
    shriek of shrapnel lips of a

foyer that is contention, white like pale cities bereaving; after Jacob in
    a parallel universe where

Isaac tears the tendon from his neck

Black Indian

BY SHONDA BUCHANAN

All my journeys begin
in North Carolina
without my knowing it;
Black Indians pushed like September crab shells
on an angry winter shore,
swept up in the storm
of Moby Dick's adventure.
The literature of us wiped and creamed
against an outcrop of colonizing rocks.
Our acorn, our buckskin, our dreaming, crushed. Corrected.
Under the weight of change, we became husks of ourselves.
We were Neusiok, fading into Coharie ghosts on a river bank.
We were redblack wolves chewing our wrists from the arm.
We fought next to the Tuscarora,
beading ourselves into a story of lush rivers
and swampland and defeat,
unaware of the coming.
Saddles and horses and silver in white mouths,
sweeping us up in their fingers like dust in the corners
of black powder pouches.
We ran. My family escaped
from that swampland in sampson county into tennessee,
to indiana,
then michigan.
Indian, Mulatto, Colored.
Black.
We planted ourselves next to the Pottawatomie
and Ottawa like cornstalks.
We grew
into a farmhouse on fire.

More Time

by Keisha-Gaye Anderson

They say you should never wake a sleepwalker. The very jolt of becoming conscious that one is actually walking through a dream might frighten the dreamer to death. Some sleepwalkers make it back to their beds, only to wake up not knowing they'd ever been sleepwalking. And in other cases, the dreamer might even feel grateful that someone woke them up before they suffered some irrevocable harm, like walking off a cliff.

I had to go all the way back to More Time to really understand something I'd always known instinctively, and to remember what my grandmother meant when she said, "Dreams don't walk straight." She knew that her dreams were another way of existing, and I believed her, even when my mother sucked her teeth at those stories about flying Africans, and men and women deflecting British bullets with their mere bodies. "Nanny wasn't the only one, you know?" she would say to me and then end with a wink. We knew that Mommy was too invested in the new life in New York to think much about the old life in More Time.

Though I was born in Brooklyn, I spent many summers with my grandmother in that little community. It wasn't on any official map of Jamaica, but all the residents agreed it was there and had always been there. It was a handful of colorful wood frame homes and a few small concrete shops, just inland from Discovery Bay, where Columbus had first set foot on the Island. Maybe it was the echo of that first contact or the memory of the Africans who staged rebellions there, but the place always seemed to hold onto a certain quiet. It was the silence that came after the last bit of blood had been wiped up, or the last too-young body buried. It permeated everything stealthily, like the gathering of dust or like the imperceptible passage of time in More Time, which is how I suppose it got its name. Mama wasn't sure. She just knew that she would never leave, and she told us so. What would she do in the cold, in New York City, with all those people? "No, sah," she would say. "Me going to stay right yah-so."

Five hundred people seemed more like a large clan than a real town anyway, and Mama liked it that way. They fished, farmed, and occasionally worked in the local hotels. The wheels of their machine turned daily in the same direction. If more people came, she said, then the 'blasted' government would find themselves down there before you blink, just to throw poor Mr. Holder and the other squatters off of their land, back there behind God's back, where the rich people had long forgotten about since the end of banana and cane.

Mama got the little plot of her land from her mother, who got it when her Scottish grandfather was feeling generous toward his bastards in his final days on Earth. I suppose the face of death can turn the tides into seemingly intractable situations and make even the boldest men consider what they will tell their maker when they finally meet him. People rarely left More Time and hardly anyone ever came.

So the summer that Zarah Dovecot came walking down the road, she looked as if she'd been shaken awake, unsure as to whether that disturbed her or made her grateful. She stepped slowly down the road, as if looking for something she'd lost. When Aunt Hyacinth saw the young woman, she almost kicked over the bucket of gungu peas that we were shelling on the verandah. "But, kiss mi neck!" She quickly went in the house to call Uncle Georgie. They both stood in the doorway, watching the tall dark woman with the short afro walk slowly down the street, looking at all of her surroundings, from the tall breadfruit tree to the pink and white bougainvillea that spilled over Aunt Hyacinth's fence. The young woman was working something out in her mind, though it didn't even seem like she was sure of what it was.

"What is it? Who is she?" I asked.

"Oh, never you mind, darlin. Nuh,worry yuself." Auntie's round cheeks plumped up as she offered me a smile of reassurance, which frightened me in its attempt to look convincing. Uncle Georgie grumbled something, and then went back into the house. Auntie walked to the front gate and began talking to the young woman, who stared at her with a mixture of recognition but aloofness. She pointed down the street and the woman walked off.

Auntie returned to the verandah and continued shelling peas, as if nothing had happened.

"So...?"

"Yes, dear?"

"Who was she?"

"She?" She sucked her teeth like she did when the neighbor's goat would continually come over and feed on the young saplings she'd recently planted in the ard. "Dat is just Zarah. Miss Dovecot gran-pickney. Was in foreign for quite some time, come to think of it."

"Mama always used to say that no one ever leaves and no one ever comes back here." I chuckled.

"May God rest her soul," Auntie said wistfully as she thought of her older sister. "Well, mi chile, weh eva it maaga, it bruk." I knew I would find out exactly what she meant later on, but I didn't press the issue.

"Where did she walk off to?"

"Miss Dovecot yard. Ovah deh-so."

"You mean that abandoned house? Is Miss Dovecot there?"

"No sah. She supposed to dead donkey years now."

"Hmm, strange. Well, maybe I'll go say hi to her tomorrow when I go out to survey the land." I fancied myself a budding organic farm owner, determined to do something productive with my grandmother's land, though Aunt Hyacinth would argue that everything was just fine as it was.

"No, you can't go over there!" Aunt Hyacinth looked at me with surprise and then restraint. The forced smile returned. "You wi meet har in time. All in due time."

The next morning, Uncle Georgie and Aunt Hyacinth were having their coco tea and bread when I heard them whispering.

"Is only a matter of time before the odda wan come," she said.

"Mi know," said Uncle Georgie.

I decided not to disturb them and take an early morning walk. Instead of taking my usual route down to the river to listen to its morning song, I was drawn by another song. The music was so near, that it seemed to originate in my head. I walked out the front gate of auntie's house and down the road, through the open field where Miss Dovecot's old house lay in the distance. The humming became louder. I knew the melody the way the body knows it needs rest, though I wasn't sure how.

As I approached the house, I noticed it was now a bright yellow and that the roof was completely repaired. Zarah seemed to be the missing piece of a puzzle that hid in plain sight, a puzzle that entangled us all. She sat very still on the verandah, having a cup of tea. Her very presence seemed to make the house breathe again. I stood at the bottom of the steps, but she still didn't look in my direction.

"Morning. I'm Selah. I'm staying with my aunt Hyacinth, just down the road. I hear you've come back home. Haven't heard of anyone coming back for more than a visit."

She nodded and smiled.

"I came here to look about starting a farm," I said, hoping to find something to talk about, and possibly form a new friendship. I loved my aunt and the town was beautiful, but I was growing a bit bored. But I was determined to make the excursion worth it, so I had to find a way to pass the time.

"That's right," said Zarah in her British accent. She seemed as if she suddenly recalled knowledge she'd forgotten. Her eyes were almost black but luminous at the same time. "You make things grow. Like Hyacinth."

"Did my aunt tell you about that yesterday? She thinks the farm is a waste of my time."

Zarah just smiled and continued to hum.

"That song you're humming, I think know that song."

"Of course you do," she said. Her stillness had in it the full weight of a storm beginning to spin itself into existence.

"So, did you have some help with the house? Looks better than I remember it."

"I just thought about it."

"Okay." This was harder than I thought. "So, how do you plan to spend this lovely day?"

"Just waiting."

"For what?"

Zarah didn't answer. She just smiled at me and handed me a white anthurium lily from the pot on the verandah and then went into the house.

When I got back to auntie's house, she was sitting on her verandah, looking resigned to a difficult task to be undertaken at any moment. Mama always said we were a family of workers, even when we were sitting still. I was starting to understand the spirit of her words, though I couldn't pinpoint why I knew this to be true.

That's when Edan walked around from behind the house. Aunt Hyacinth sighed when she saw him. He was very white, with blue eyes and raven hair, what some would call Black Irish. He wore a British Navy uniform. He looked through us at first, and then at the flower that I was holding. He looked back up at me, his eyes luminescent like Zarah's. I felt a spark dart up my spine and the briefest déjà vu took over my senses.

Edan turned and walked out of the yard as quietly as he had emerged and headed toward the Dovecot house. I placed the lily on the table and sat next to my aunt.

"Miss Dovecot did love a soldier one time," said Aunt Hyacinth. "To see it...It was like heaven touch earth. But di more heaven touch earth, di more earth get confuse. Heaven nuh suppose to deh pon earth."

"I don't understand."

"Look there," said my aunt, as she pointed to the table. A bunch of lilies of every

color cascaded from a glass vase.

"I was just thinking of an arrangement like that."

"Then, you understand. And soon you will understand why dem can't stay."

Edan and Zarah moved into the old house and the people of More Time didn't pay them much mind, except the old people, who half-remembered Miss Dovecot and looked at the lovers with a tickling sensation, an expectation that something was supposed to happen, though they weren't sure what. But since it was true that no one really ever left the town, they made space for them and also let them have their space. To do otherwise would have been like cutting off a finger.

The couple kept to themselves, didn't speak to anyone, and just kept each other's company day in and day out. The old house they lived in seemed to transform a little bit each day from a ramshackle state to a brand-new dwelling. It seems like every few days, a new fruit plant or flowering bush would appear in their yard until the whole property carried the wafting sweet fragrances of nectar and syrup.

Then, the people of More Time began to see the glow. That's when Aunt Hyacinth began to shake her head more and more. It started with young people. Zarah and Edan would walk to the little store together and they would both smile at the schoolchildren on the road. Smitty's boy saw it first. That glow in their eyes, something beyond time, something in everything and everyone, and in himself. That's when he remembered that he could fly. The boy floated up in the air, dropped his books, and took off into the valley, laughing all the time.

Then there was Carlene, the shopkeeper's daughter. She said she saw that glow in their eyes, and then around their bodies. She thought about going down to the beach and then blinked her eyes, and she was there. Carlene popped in and out of so many places that people weren't startled anymore.

All of the people of More Time felt the glow tingle up their spine until they became the ultimate manifestations of themselves and expressed their desires in ways that the rest of the island wouldn't understand, but would also never know, because More Time and its people were barely a blip on the radar.

I began my farming by just picturing the crops. Pretty soon, corn and callaloo exploded their plots, and naseberries grew as big as soccer balls. I missed my return flight home and usually kept the red dirt between my hands and toes.

Aunt Hyacinth didn't say much. She just kept shaking her head. "Heaven cyaan meet the earth," she would say. But the last straw for her was when the government officials came to More Time, like rodents sniffing a trail of crumbs.

"Same thing I tell you," She said to me as we sat on the veranda eating a bowl of mangos I'd just grown that morning.

"What can they really do?"

"What they did to Miss Dovecot. Dem bury har under dat same house di last time. Di time she did bring di English chap here. Must be 1850? Mi nuh quite remember. But dem times especially, yu couldn't love who you want to love, even ef it was to love yuself."

"Dem ole African know demself looong time. Dem knoa seh di bakra live in sleep and dat ah di ongle life dem cyan have. But di ole African dem 'low dem fi believe she dem ah boss, just fi di sake a living. Sleepwalk betta dan dead. But den, nuttin nuh really dead fi true. And dem African know dat too. So, dem nuh worry demself too much bout it."

"But Miss Dovecot have a fiya heart. Dat gyal just couldn't walk through life with one eye shut. She love the man. Di man lov har. Dem love fill up di fruit trees and bring dung di river in di sun hot. Di bakra dem know how that dis kinda love, it love change tings, mek flowa bloom, mek people fi fly. But dem nuh know di ting itself, and dat is what vex dem. Dat is always what vex dem. Dat is why dem bury dat ooman underneath that house. But see, she come back. And the man come back too. Every day is just more time, but ah nuh nuttin, still."

"We here know seh we haffi sleep fi live in bakra world, so we walk with one eye shut. But Zarah, she sleep walking with all eyes open, and to bring dat world here, it just can't work mi chile. It just can't work."

"Here comes one," I said.

The brown-skinned man wore a dapper linen suit and carried a folder filled with papers.

"Excuse me, Miss."

Aunt Hyacinth continued to bite into her mango.

"We are here to see about some squatters in that yard." He motioned to behind the house. "Do you know anything about that?"

I looked at Aunt Hyacinth. She looked at the armed private security who traveled with the official, waiting near the Range Rover. She sucked her teeth. "Enough ah dis."

She began to breathe hard with her eyes closed and a low rumbling shook the house. The shaking got more vigorous, so I held onto the iron railing. Then it was as if a giant hand came down from the sky and snatched the men away one by one. But it wasn't just the men, it was also each and every house in More Time. One by one, they were pulled up into the air, and in a 'pop!' they vanished.

I saw the Dovecot house rise in the air. Edan and Zarah sat on the verandah, unmoved. Little by little, they began to glow, brighter and brighter, until there were no more bodies, just shining lights that floated up around the house. The lights came over to aunt Hyacinth, who still concentrated with her eyes shut as our own house floated up in the air. The lights touched her head and she smiled and jerked as if an electric jolt ran through her body. Then, we vanished.

I fell into a deep sleep, the deepest I'd ever had. And when I woke up, I was back in Brooklyn. At my front door was a package waiting for me, from Aunt Hyacinth. It was a black cake, made with rum-soaked fruits from my fruit trees. In her note, she said, "We will always have More Time, but now, just settle, Selah, and walk with one eye open. I am your loving aunt, Hyacinth."

More Time still isn't on any map, but the people agreed it was there, and were really happy to have woken up, even if they decided to go back to sleep for the time being.

"Tap, Tap"

BY APRIL GARDNER

Caroline had not visited her Southern roots since she left Longview, Texas in 1975, but a supernatural incident caused by a supernatural force called her home. Her baby brother Timothy had died. When arriving home, all Caroline could focus on was, "Not tonight!" Those two words rang like a resounding gong in her ear, even above the weeping of her grandmother, aunts, and sisters. Extended family came and paid their respects until nightfall. When the relatives that lived in town went home, the house fell quiet, and those that no longer lived in the house drew sticks to see who would have to stay in the house overnight, or who of the out-of-owners got to stay with another relative. Unfortunately for Caroline, she drew the short stick, along with her older sister Doris.

"I will stay in Timothy's old room," said Caroline to Doris. "And I will stay right down here by the front door," exclaimed Doris.

The house had remained exactly as it was when Caroline left…old. The smell of wet air permeated the walls, and every piece of furniture was exactly where it was supposed to be. At the front door, one could take in the entire house. A rocking chair sat by the fireplace, that only Caroline's grandmother had sat in. The couch was five feet away from the rocking chair and was still decorated by the hand-stitching efforts of old Native hands, and a large window took the place off the wall that adorned the front door. All but the upstairs was present to any visitor. As Caroline began to climb the stairs, she remembered why relatives drew straws. One had to know the creaking steps, to ensure not tripping up. The steps were made of an unidentifiable plastic and sat higher than any set of stairs Caroline had come into contact with. Since her grandmother required darkness when one was not present in a room, and since one had no business on the stairwell but to travel up and down stairs, one had to make the trip from one floor to the next in pitch black.

Timothy's room was on the right-hand side, only two feet from the stairwell. Caroline went in. She did not miss her brother, because he always seemed to be in trouble, and they had not spoken in years. As Caroline laid her body down on Timothy's old bed, and lay her head on her brother's old pillow, she felt rested, then, a "tap" on her foot. The feeling did not process.

Two minutes later, a "tap, tap" on the same foot. Sleep no longer had Caroline's attention. She could not open her eyes, fearing what she would see, or not see. Caroline could only think to retreat to under the covers, and so she did. As Caroline began to pull the covers over her head, she felt a weight on the sheets that came from the direction of her feet. Someone had sat down! Caroline immediately ran out of the dark room, down the dark stairwell, and into the pullout bed where her sister Doris was laying. Doris sat up as Caroline climbed into bed, and both said in unison, "not tonight!"

black girl magic

BY NOMAD THE POET

as i swim in the celestial pools
that reside within my hoops,
i pluck an unsaid prayer
from my teeth.

it talks of the love
that's embedded deep
within my skin,
the wisdom that is caught
between my kinks.

sings praises of the meadows
that reside,
where my thighs divide.
calls my fields sacred ground–

where both men
and earth
collide.

Laments,

to the painting of my bones
a deep and vicious red;

the color of the diaspora
that my people have bled.

whispers the longings
of both saints and sinners,

how they confess-
they desire my temple
be their next conquest.

how they pray late at night
to swim with their Divine.
ignorant to the light
that lies behind My eyes

Sistah

by Richard May III

A Quest to Appease the Ancestors

BY LINDA TRICE

A young woman walked quietly through the forest that was unknown to her. In appearance she seemed like any other female of her age. She wore a long sleeved tee shirt which had the logo of the college where she was a student of anthropology and folklore. Her face was summer tanned. What marked her as one on a quest to satisfy the Ancestor was her hair - long, thick braids held tight by leather strings and strips of blood red cloth.

She had always lived with and been raised by the grandmother who sent her on this spiritual journey. It was the custom among their African ancestors to give the first born child to the grandmother. That child would live with her grandmother and devote her life to caring for her. And thus it had been.

Grandmother told the young woman that an African ancestor, a high priest, escaped from enslavement in the Carolinas and came to Florida where he was given sanctuary by the Seminole. He married into the fold and had children by his wife who some called a shaman because of her knowledge of herbs and roots. Their children had children by others in the group, some African, some Seminole.

But Andrew Jackson, Wiley Thompson, Thomas Jessup and others demanded the Africans return to perpetual slavery. Their beloved children would be taken from them and sold. The Seminole were told to walk to reservations in Oklahoma and leave their lands for the whites. The United States government called it "Removal".

The Seminole fought. Many died. The army kept the survivors away from the dead so the bodies of some, such as the Ancestor and most of his children were left on the ground to rot.

Thus the quest of the young woman was to find Seminole Mound, the site of the massacre and once there to set things right.

Her grandmother sent her on this spiritual journey with sacred herbs and knowledge of the chants. Grandmother made the journey when she was a young woman and planted Jimson weed in the sacred site. And by the plant and its white trumpet like flowers the young woman would know she had arrived at the Seminole Mound.

The young woman was not bothered by the buzzing insects. Her knowledge of the swamps protected her from poisonous snakes, alligators and other living forms which so plague the Northerners who moved to Florida.

At last she came to the area, but as her grandmother had predicted, it was no longer uninhabited. A run down cabin sat on top of the small mound.

She waited until she was sure no one was around, performed her ceremony, then slipped back into the forest and home. The deed was done.

Cassandra approached Wiley Jessup's dilapidated house with trepidation. She tried to shake the feeling off. Locals said the mound was cursed and wouldn't go near the place. They saw ghosts and strange lights at night. Scientists from the University said it was just swamp gas.

She thought of the legend and just as quickly discounted it. That's why the artist had been able to buy the property so cheaply from her agency. After all, the area abounded with wild tales of the supernatural. The Swamp Ape was the regional version of Big Foot. Sensational media placed South Florida within the Bermuda Triangle and claimed the lost continent of Atlantis was off the coast.

Cassandra leaned against a nearly dead tree and appraised the property. Bleak. Dirt. Jimson weed was the only plant and it was struggling to survive. Locals called it the Devil's Trumpet because of the triangle shaped flowers. Wiley's property was just a worthless piece of land. The only use it was good for was just what Wiley was putting it to, a retreat from the world and he had surely done that.

Minutes later she was sitting next to the painter in his living room. The burly man was dressed in his usual attire - torn denim shorts and a tee shirt with the arms ripped off. His clothes were faded and splattered with paint.

"Really Wiley, I worry about you," Cassandra said. "You have such artistic talent, but you're alone too much. You should get out more, be with people."

He ignored her. He was too busy admiring his newest work, a self-portrait. Although he hadn't hung it yet, it was large enough for him to enjoy as it lay against the wall. "What do you think?"

"It captures your essence," she said. "It's the real you, the bushy eyebrows, your rugged looks."

He nodded, agreeing with her.

"It's different from your other works, 'County Courthouse', 'Baseball Training Camp'. Those are gritty, yet they capture the essence and culture of Beneva County, of much of South Florida in fact. They're realistic, earthy and so ... so you."

He smiled, looking at the painting not at the woman.

She put her now empty beer can on the floor and stood. Obviously he just wanted someone to admire his latest work. "Got to go now," she said.

When she reached the door, she looked back at him. Cassandra was about to say something but realized that Wiley was still intently savoring his latest work.

She let herself out, got into her car and drove off. She had her own life to lead.

There was an opening that night. Wiley's agent strenuously urged him to attend. A Miami collector was interested in some of Wiley's more expensive works but refused to buy them until he had gotten to know the artist. Wine poured freely as usual.

Afterwards the collector insisted that Wiley and the agent accompany him to The Quay for bourbon and jazz. The collector insisted upon buying "just one more round", then another and another.

As Wiley pulled into his isolated house a few minutes before midnight, he realized he'd forgotten to eat dinner. The wine and the bourbon made him clutch his stomach.

Instead of going into the kitchen to get something to eat, he went to the self-portrait. He studied it intently, his hands on his hips, his legs spread. Cassandra was right. It did capture his essence.

He looked up past it to a portrait he'd painted of a former girlfriend, a dancer with a ballet troupe. It was unlike most of his work. He had done it in pale pinks and ivory, colors that reminded him of her soft gentleness.

The figure was intent on tying her pink slipper, but gently and slowly her head came up.

She turned around, stared at Wiley and stepped out of the painting. Standing quite still, now five feet tall, she moved into a corner and twirled round and around.

To the left of the ballerina, the "Riverview High School Band" began to play. A uniformed tuba player marched off the painting, followed by drummers, bagpipe players, then the entire band. All two hundred and fifty of them marched with precise steps into the bedroom.

The surf in Wiley's "Siesta Key Beach" began to splash. Some of the bathers spread their blankets in front of Wiley's wall. High school girls started a volleyball game.

Wiley stared speechless, horrified, but the wine, bourbon and the late hour overtook him. He slumped down onto the blanket of the Siesta Key bathers and passed out.

In the corner, the ballerina still twirled.

Wiley woke in his bed. He didn't know how he got there. He didn't remember removing his clothes but there they were, his shirt and best jeans, tangled in a heap on the floor near his good sandals.

He shook his head again remembering last night. He stared at the painting in front of him. "The Bridge Players" silently inspected their cards. Next to it, another of his works showed diners at a seaside restaurant. The patrons were seated, their cigarettes and coffee cups posed in midair. All the other paintings in the bedroom were as they should be, still.

It must have been the wine, he thought as he showered and dressed.

Not totally convinced that it had only been a bad dream, he inspected the paintings in the living room. The ballerina was still bending over her pink slipper. The band was in their state of blessed stillness.

Wiley shook his head again. It had to have been the wine. From now on he was sticking strictly to beer.

Soon the house was filled with the aroma of freshly brewed coffee and the sounds of Wiley whistling as he began hanging his selfportrait. An hour later, he made a sandwich with the last roll and whatever cold cuts he had left.

He groaned. He'd have to go into town later. He hated the nosy townspeople, the friendly kids at the checkout. Too friendly. He came out here to paint, not to make friends.

There was another opening that night. It was so crowded that Wiley didn't get a chance to have more than two glasses of wine. They had no beer. His agent had insisted he come. His agent often had lousy ideas. This was one.

Wiley approached his house with trepidation that night. As he stood in front of the door, he thought he heard music.

He smiled to himself. Of course. Probably some kids parked a way back doing something they shouldn't in the back seat of a banged up old car. Music carried out here.

As soon as he entered the house, he got a can of cold beer. Savoring a swallow, he sat down on his sofa, his feet up and enjoyed his paintings.

When he went to get another beer he patted his "Pickers in an Orange Grove" hanging outside the kitchen and caressed his "Circus Winter Headquarters" hanging on the opposite wall.

Then he heard a caressing female voice gently call his name.

His head jerked towards the window, then the television.

There was no one outside.

The television was blank.

He shook his head and took another sip of beer.

It was then he heard the sound. Like a music box. Soft and tinkling.

He looked up. The ballerina was standing before him, smiling. She pirouetted towards a corner and twirled round and around.

The two hundred and fifty member Riverview High School Band played their instruments and marched through the room. The animals from "County Fair" began bleating and weaving through the musicians' feet. The noise was deafening.

A man with an orange for a face came in from the bedroom. "Come," the man spoke.

Mesmerized by the horror and with an insatiable curiosity, Wiley followed the faceless man, the band and the parade.

He watched, fascinated as the creatures and the people miniaturized and flowed into their respective frames.

Wiley wheeled around as the person who had led him at the end of the parade into the bedroom, shrank and floated into a frame above the bed.

Then Wiley noticed another painting his selfportrait which he had just hung. As he stared, he felt an odd sensation. He was becoming smaller. He was soaring through the air, towards the self-portrait, the image of an artist with a white Devil's Trumpet flower dangling from his hand.

People still claim to see ghostly lights and hear plaintive cries. Researchers at the University just as adamantly discount it all as local superstition.

The end

Historical Note: Andrew Jackson's invasion of Florida led to the First Seminole War. The Removal Act was passed in 1830. Seminoles were forced to leave Florida and walk to Oklahoma. Wiley Thompson was in charge of the Removal. Thomas Jessup, the commander of all U.S. troops in Florida during the Second Seminole War said about the Seminole, "The country can be rid of them only by exterminating them."

THESE BLACK BODIES ARE
MINDFUL

No matter how obsessed you've been with your own vanishing,
there will always be someone who wants you whole.

—Hanif Abdurraqib

Cashier

by Stephani Maari Booker

Stand on the black rubber mat that's supposed to save long-flattened feet. Hold back the shaking tongue because it wants to lash out at the customer with multiple coupons on a smartphone that has to be scanned, then explained. Sorry, this one won't work on these items in that way. The buyer responds with a terse voice and a hard stare. Hold back the eyes from running away to sit on the grey aisle floors, tap on the red "Clearance" signs and brush against the rainbow of bath towels. Take a swallow, open your mouth: "Let me call a sales lead to help you." Manager mollifies with a paper flyer discount. A frown turned upside down, the purchaser exits the store. The manager grants permission to retreat. Run to the break room, hide from the shoppers, and hope to be sent to the solitude of backstock.

Anxiety rings
up concessions; privilege
orders submission.

Worst Case Scenario

by Jennifer Maritza McCauley

I've mourned my life before I've died
It's pitiful, but that's the way I go about it.

I imagine the car crushed before it drives
I see the plane mid-crash before it soars.
I curse you for leaving before you arrive.

What to do with these imaginings?
It's easy to see how I'd tumble into fall
What to do with this grim thinking?
Without effort, I can't grow in love

To cure the mind, I think of a field
Reckless in its immobility and waving flora.
I smell sun tucked under unwintered blossoms
I imagine only that field until disaster fades.

Mental Health

BY JENNIFER MARITZA McCAULEY

On a new afternoon, I awake
And the mass wakes with me.

I can't see it but it's large.
I can't see it but it's fond of gooey gab.
I can't see it but it's boulder-heavy,
I can't see it, but I know I can't get around
it's damning size.

It squats on my chest and takes a shit.
It squats on my back and twerks into me,
It squats on my head and its ass is on my eyes,

This mass has no love for me, that's certainly true.

On a cold afternoon, I awake
And greet the mass.
It says *fuck you* and I go about my business.

I tuck the mass in deep so I can't see its shape.
I tuck the mass in my bloodstream and hope it dies.

On a different night, I forget the mass exists.
This is how I go about these days:
Battling for the next moment, knowing
I don't care if the mass is crushing my neck,
Or if it ever existed at all.

Nightmares

by Ginger Galloway

Pain-filled memories of a life I have not lived haunt me when I close
my eyes
To bring me alive in shadows of evening light.
The moon has become my companion.
She tells me secrets in languages I do not speak.
A chorus of stars nods. Unwitting scribes of blackness.
Love and pain are kin in this place. Broken fingernails caress bruised
knuckles embrace.

Curtains billow into the room like trails of taints
Images of keloid skin echo the piercing rip of leather straps.
A coyote calls to the heavens in a song only the ancestors can
understand.
My lips do not obey the desire to respond to the wickedness of it all.
Prayers stay trapped in my mind where they resonate until the sun
peeks in
to see if I have survived the night.

Night in Fort Pierce

by Jennifer Maritza McCauley

The night has a pretty good attitude.
Star-stripped and rushing,
I imagine a librettist
Singing complexities to the
Black-blue spread above.

The sand is flat and vague-looking.
The ocean is roaring fierce.
The pelicans squat, huddle, and rest.
Cars complain softly.

It's so quiet it's cacophonous
The night says I've got this fine.

I can't sleep but I absorb
The black air chattering.

I can't sleep but the wind
Cradles me alive.

for aswad

BY PAMELA PETÉ

He HE
   loud   sudden   out of nowhere
brows furrow lips turn down
a comical if not so tragic toothy grin
gradually   separates his face

bank customers turn concerned

shhh   *before they kick us out*
his mind racing around finding no exit
help me
       please
               he whispers

desperation spills from his eyes

can't get out   he doesn't know how

do you think i have mental issues

charged collect   the call   i pay

                      another courtroom   another case
                      his lips form a smile   that fails his eyes
                      looking through me   pleading *Nana*
                      cuffed in back   as he's lead away

                      He HE   fills the silence

                      his keyless clueless confinement
                      surrenders him   to the weighing
                      yet life-saving lock ups   lock downs
                      propelling his spiral implosion
                          help me
                                help   *him*

Sleeping Beauty

BY NAYSHA COKER

Her skin has a smooth amber hue
Adorn With overalls hospital blue
On the right arm there could be traced
A single scar Where nourishment was placed

An experience that's a lingering effect
Created instability in the mind that never left

Each thought an empty plot
Land an attempt at cognition that had trouble
Being brought to fruition
In this place exist
No rock for lying or cushion for coping
Nor even greenery for acres around
A mental field
Her inheritance the fertile ground
Without a single finger
Browned, from tilling the soil

When Voices Come Calling

BY ERIC DEVAUGHNN

(they will not smile nor whisper soft&kind)
my brother—weary of the illness—chose
to bounce&bleed through worn out, broken soles
which matched, too well, his all-too-tender mind

he left his home, bound for northern borders
the siren call of canada, just loud
enough to drown the cackles of the crowd
nipping at his heels—he found no quarter.

five days into his trudge, in roadside brush
a mountain ranger found him nearly dead
when momma got the call at church, we rushed
to stand—bloom&bouquet—around his bed

so grateful for the living bones adorning:
what better way to spend Thanksgiving morning?

Wander through the Mess

BY KARIN PLEASANT

Wandering feels luxurious when I'm embracing suspension and not caring for a moment or two where I'll land.

Daydreaming has been a place of solace filled with un-danced dances and an overflow of rhythms. I wish I could stay suspended and lost in my imagination.

But wandering can be dangerous, detaching too much from what's happening around me and missing connections that could reveal what I've desired most, a place to call home.

Conflict is constant in my body and mind with aches I can't soothe and pain pulsing across my forehead because I can't decipher in a digital world what impact means when clicks decide what and who is necessary and valuable.

Unbalanced inquiry of how to disturb the peace others are comfortable with, I stand in mental quicksand waiting for a sign.

Harnessing anxiety, grief, and frustration, I'm afraid all I'll remember is failure. A tilt of the head forces a change in focus, highlighting the loneliness of the time in my head.

I see I'm trying to learn to accept myself more than any social condition.

The constant confusion is meant to be distracting and debilitating, but I want to believe I can wander with purpose and try to convince myself that I'm enough.

Will a Flower Bloom from a Multi-Tasking Pain?

by Jacquese Armstrong

No flowers have bloomed in this concrete jungle for a while. The only soil that is left is devoid of its rich nutrients, its emollients. In every instance, a color tries to court a budding plant it is retracted in some form...

The body politic, after almost four years of aggressive divisionism rhetoric, is drained. Our defenses are down. It is no wonder we are the world's epicenter for coronavirus activity.

In my personal life, my defenses have been almost depleted also, after 39 years of living with a thought and mood disorder where nothing is as it appears. At 59, my body politic, the individual parts, and limbs are rebelling against themselves.

Entering the pandemic shelter-in-place mode in March 2020, we were all already drained. Life had been a rushing multi-tasking over-scheduled mess for quite some time. Even in shelter-in-place our lives were still seemingly progressing at the speed of light. And it seemed that every step of the way a calamity of the body politic collided with thoughts of my past situations and produced PTSD moments, because of the liquidity of days spent in solitary.

I witnessed horrific parts of my life flash like lightning the entire quarantine...

Like that small hollow space, though in my head, with a front room, bedroom, bath, and kitchenette, which is a warp in time, my twilight zone. The place where I lost my world. The place where I lost my mind.

The pandemic inconveniently made my present apartment feel like the first, as I was chained to it, back against the door, smoking three packs of cigarettes daily. Though not presently chained by psychosis, paranoia, and the confusion of delusion. Nevertheless, I was chained.

At neither time in my life did I roam freely?

So, Trauma gangstered his way into my space once more and I had to mourn the 20-year-old me again. [author], the chemical engineering junior whose dream candle was snuffed out before it could get a good flicker against darkness.

But, since I was no longer her, I had an AK-47 for Trauma, ready and waiting. He had unmercifully murdered my engineering career. And now, among other things, I create expressive arts workshops to foster mental wellness. So, I amped up my game and my arsenal.

Thankfully, the arts community had decided to come together from all directions and offer free workshops which I hoarded. I zoomed all over. I answered every poetry and writing call, kept more than one art journal, and a gratitude journal, did daily devotions, and started developing online alternatives for my workshops.

I was not going back to the sinisterly oppressive environment of psychosis that had restricted my air until I nearly lost my life.

But then Trauma returned and reared his ugly head again because then I saw him...

He had his knee in George Floyd's throat, stopping the airflow, knowingly. He was casual. His hands were in his pockets, a non-committal look on his face, no remorse. When I witnessed this execution, I snapped. It was the proverbial straw for me from over 400 years of grave injustice, horrific deeds, and heinous crimes served to me by America. My ancestors do live on inside of me.

In that moment, as I wrote a poem to free my emotions, I found the rage was exhausted. It had shown up consistently for centuries, but today, I found it exhausted; tired. I had just paid homage to the hijacked lives of Ahmaud Arbery and Breonna Taylor in a four-page poem that took it back to the ship because nothing done to a black person in America is an isolated case. No matter how much they try to get you to believe it or taunt you for playing a card they 4 published in a press passed down to them from their privileged families, it is not isolated but another dot to connect.

But there he was, casual as the wind on a resort beach, with his knee in Mr. Floyd's throat for more than 8 minutes, in broad daylight with no regard for a video or crowd.

Like Mr. Floyd, I went numb. And at that moment, the numbness disoriented my power. There was nothing I could do for this man or any man I knew whose skin was of that beautiful hue. And that was this man's mindset. This man with his knee in the throat of a Black American. He set about to take a life because he thought there would be no consequence, no repercussions. In that context, with the recent kill and cover-up of Mr. Arbery and the brutal invasion and murder of Ms. Taylor, you would think the government-sanctioned killing would recede with the whole world looking. But the turtle's pace genocide continued with the spineless shooting of Rayshard Brooks in the back three times and the tearful memories of countless others. I don't think that I'm in a time warp as some would say, because I know the killing has never stopped.

Thoughts clash-collided in my head and trauma consumed my body again. Don't ever let anyone tell you that mental health trauma, with regard to the effects of racism on a black body, is not real. Don't ever let anyone tell you that this trauma cannot be passed through generations.

Numbness and powerlessness were the two dictators informing my every move for 24 years. It was as if someone had placed a knee on my neck and taken my breath, my hopes, my dreams, and my potential.

For 24 years I had no control over the constant chatter in my head. In addition, I had to deal with and still occasionally deal with a very pronounced paranoia, delusional thinking, and depression. They diagnosed this as a schizoaffective disorder when I was in my twenties. And being witness to Mr. Floyd's murder, triggered that emotional pain again which produced the numbness that led to feelings of powerlessness.

My life got hijacked just as I was about to realize my first large goal; there was nothing I could do about that. Sometimes, I am the walking dead. Ahmaud's life was hijacked. Breonna's life was hijacked and so too were George Floyd's and Rayshard's and so many more. But they will never return.

Having that power inadequacy feeling again, revealed something to me though. Because I had no power to control the voices showing up in my head, I decided to stop showing up. I decided not to play full out in my own life. It hurts too badly to lose over and over again through no fault of your own, because of a mental illness, or the collective effect of a knee in the back of someone's neck, or the paranoia that precedes being hunted down,. The surprise attack of psychosis invades your mind until you want to disconnect your head or the collective psychological effect of the 6 surprise invasions and attack of bullets on brown skin until you're more than dead (or so it would seem.)

A loss of power affects individuals differently. For some, the shifting goes into overdrive; like, how dare you tell me what I can't do. But the thing is, most of us will start out this way. The question is: How long can you hold your breath while running double time until opportunity and justice reward you?

How long can you hold your breath while you output 300% to the norm and get less than 100% expected back?

How long can you hold your breath until housing and healthcare are made affordable for you?

How long can you hold your breath until adequate food stores and transportation make their way to your neighborhood?

I asked myself how long I could hold my breath until I got a fair shake at a career and my mental health held up at the same time.

After 10 years, I dropped any semblance of social life. After 15 years, I no longer dreamed lofty dreams and set them as goals. I just wanted to work a job, any job, and keep it and afford it. After 20 years of holding my breath, I went blind. But I kept showing up and looking for work.

How long can you hold your breath? And can you maintain your dignity with a lack of oxygen when people are consistently cutting down trees?

In this country, I have three strikes against me. I have a "mental illness," which I deem a pejorative term. I live on the poverty level, and I am a person of color.

Although 59, and still unable to hold a full-time "traditional" job and hold "it" together, I am still working on the income part by trying to use my skills as a consultant. Yes, you can't keep some of us from lofty dreams set to goals for too long. And I'll be damned if I let someone tell me that I'm inferior because my skin color is so appealing. The thing that messed with my mind though was the stigma associated with "mental illness," even by my own brothers and sisters. In the end, this fight was my redemption. It brought me back to sea level. It brought me back from zombie-land, the land of the walking dead.

With so many different walks and cultures rallying the cry of no stigma and working to alleviate it, surely, I thought, we could win this one. And at least I wasn't born into this fight. 8 Imagine being born into a fight of over 400 years in which nobody gives a damn about how you phrase and rephrase concepts over centuries, although you have the highest moral ground.

I was given black history books to read before I was 5. Although I read novels, they were written on my comprehension level of course. As a child, I reasoned that black people had to be superior given the deprivations America bestowed upon us, and yet we had so many iconic activists, authors, poets, inventors, and entrepreneurs. White people surely got it wrong, or were they jealous? These were my reasonings at 5. I must say at 59, I am still perplexed by the situation.

And yet, some still wonder why the protest. Some even profess to say how dare you; you're un-American. In a sense they're right. The true America is a thief. A thief that stole land and futures, cultures, and mother tongues; and refuses to this day to give even the dignity and respect due in return, over 400 years later. Personally, I'm expecting more.

My parents and I were a part of the last wave of the great migration from the south. We made a home in Akron, OH in a modest house in a segregated neighborhood one block from public housing and one block from a public school that was closed to our neighborhood before I went to kindergarten because of redistricting. I ended up starting school about four blocks away in another neighborhood. I was six in the spring of 1968.

The corner store next to our house was set on fire. I remember the fire trucks and the national guard riding through the neighborhood. The memories are sketchy; however, it is another trauma revisited. Mainly traumatic, for the fact that in more than 50 years we still have not impressed America with the fact that Black Lives Matter.

So, this is where we are, and from the present American way of rushing, over-scheduling, and multi-tasking everything, there had to be another fallout. That fallout is the multi-tasking of pain. And we, as people of color, of course, bear the brunt of it. We have always multi-tasked everything.

We get to bear the everyday pain of living life in the modern day, as everyone does. We get to bear the highest percentage of COVID-19 infiltration and the pain and. grief of losing loved ones that go with that. We get to bear the pain of knowing or not knowing we have been singled out for any given thing from working to living for our skin color; forcing us to live in a state of environmentally induced paranoia. We get to bear the pain of a family, each time we see one of our brothers or sisters gunned down, choked, body-slammed, etc. from child to adult, by police who cloak themselves in a government sanction and go scot-free.

We get to bear the pain of our history, when ancestors cry out for justice, which we have not been able to give them yet.

Blood pours in the streets every day, and yet most say it is non-existent while at the same time, telling us to clean up our footprints.

But we show up for work. We give the 300% that is expected of us to get wages that are not comparable to our white counterparts; we still protest. And we do this even though we are tired and exhausted from multi-tasking pain.

It is on this ground I stood as I watched a knee casually placed in a black man's, George Floyd's, neck. I pause to cover my eyes and take the breath he was not afforded.

In the following days as brothers and sisters took to the streets once again, I saw something I didn't expect to see because the days before had left me feeling very old and cynical.

The young started leading with the fiery tongues of ancestors. Americans of all hues gathered to protest. I saw some policemen join the march. I saw some white women form a human chain in front of black protesters. I found that white friends I never had a race conversation with before actually understood the history. This shocked me, but it gave me a dose of hope also.

I wondered if just as I was renewed by the multicultural, multi-socioeconomic level fight for stigma going on in the mental health community if America could see the beginning of 11 redemptions in this moment. I knew at that moment it would all come down to what happened in this tumultuous angst-ridden time in which our 2020 presidential elections had come to check up on us.

For me, the coming together was a little plant budding its way through a crack in the concrete.

Now that the elections are over and more mischief has ensued, and up and down are no longer distinct definitions to almost half of our country, and by some miracle, I still see that little plant. It's called hope. The question is, will it survive this next go-round?

THESE BLACK BODIES ARE
ENLIGHTENED

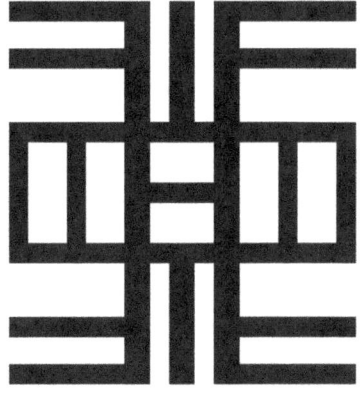

The paradox of education is precisely this
as one begins to become conscious
one begins to examine the society
in which he is being educated.
— James Baldwin

Teaching Artist

BY AKUA LEZLI HOPE

She will forget me
I hope she does, forgive
for having failed her
for raising, rousing her to express
her truth before the powerbroker
who held the keys to the gates of hell and reason
who decided her fate for the year
that makes a small forever

She had crafted a clever shell
pretending to be a land tortoise
when she was of the sea
doing her best to be Barbie and Valley girl
among Northern Appalachian wannabes and nearly gones
her small bright darkness made mud instead of ebony

I didn't consider with what care
she must torture her hair
chooses the too-short skirt
cultivates a coterie of blonde buddies
how they huddle together and flirt

She matches their shrill giggles for giggle
meets invitations to read aloud, to share
with firm refusal, though others dare
Until, working indifferent magic,
I summon her forth heedlessly

Forgetting we are in a town whose children flee
This experiment, injected content
cracked eggs, a quick scramble
on its wrong side, in its worse junior high
far from its middle or tiny, shiny, black patch

I dismiss how no place is offered
for my coat or tools or handouts or gifts
We are both alone among enemies
of invention, progress, discovery

I hope she forgets what happens next,
later, in the hall her teacher, a tired
aging, red-swelled bulk, blocks exit
yells, 'so you can think', pulls her fragile hair,
shakes her short slender frame
I pray that if scarred, she knows
that dragon's flame was pyrrhic praise,
backward compliment, bleak acknowledgment
better, she forgets, but remembers the lesson,
something about freedom of expression
and power of one's own words.

Lil Deb

BY DUAN KELLUM

Inside the Principal's Office

by Ginger Galloway

When I showed up in your office you smiled brightly. You thought that your teeth would change my focus. Your demeanor was a far cry from the frustration I was met with on the phone declaring the malady, the new thing that my son has done to offend the teachers that don't look like him. The one who determined at the beginning of the year that he would not do well in your class. The brown children's faces lacing the wall, white ones full of your teeth, beaming and free.

Spelling Bee

BY GEORGE HAMMONS

You don't know how hard it is being a class dummy
The glazed eyes of team members
who would rather be part of a group project,
with anyone other than you.

The teacher circling
question poised like a dagger
while you shrink
trying to avoid eye contact
just one of the many survival mechanisms
that a lifetime of wrong answers has endowed

Imagine the shock
down to three of us
and the room stunned that
I'm still standing

When the next word comes
I misspell it
on purpose
The room *gasps*

But as I take my seat, I tell myself that
there is an order
to how things
should be
coming third

is safe
a fluke
and thus
within the imaginations
of those who see this day-dreamy kid
with some attention issues as
a dummy

Being Jean Toomer in America

BY CALVIN SHAW

Jean Toomer was an great American poet born as Nathan Pinchback Toomer in Washington D.C. in 1894. Toomer wrote many poems, plays, and short stories throughout his successful career. He was the product of a mixed couple, and he suffered from the idea of living a life among the African American and white-American communities.

Kenneth Rexroth is a poet who heavily studied many poetic techniques and used them in his writings. Critics say reading his short poems is like reading poems his works over a 40-year period. Some refer to Rexroth as a historian of poetry and his use of mixing techniques and not excluding them is like what Toomer believes in when it relates to his idea of being an American, excluding the labels white or African.

Kenneth Rexroth stated, "Jean Toomer is the first poet to unite folk culture and the elite culture of the white avant-garde, and he accomplishes this difficult task with considerable success. He is, without doubt, the most important Black poet." I strongly disagree with this statement by Rexroth because Toomer was a man that did not identify himself as a Black man. To crown him as the most important Black poet would be a personal insult to him and many poets of color that loved their rich heritage.

Regarding the other declaration about culture mixing, Toomer took advantage of the folk and elite cultures by leveraging their lifestyles and writing works that relate to their everyday life. He not only caused rifts among the cultures in his work, but he is what some would call a "culture vulture."

Jean Toomer suffered with his racial identity from a young man until the day he died. Going into further detail about this crisis, one will examine an article by Rudolph P Byrd and Henry Louis Gates Jr. entitled, "Jean Toomer's Conflicted Racial Identity." Jean Toomer rarely spoke publicly about being a black man in America until he feels as though there is a hardship, he faces because of the color of his skin.

At the age of 27, Toomer wrote a letter to a young black woman he desired, "We who have Negro blood in our veins, who are culturally and emotionally the most removed from Puritan tradition, are its most tenacious supporters" (Byrd & Gates Jr.). As the authors state, this is one of the rare instances where Toomer brings up his black ancestry in public or privately. This shows the reader that Toomer was fine connecting to his roots only to please the woman he was pursuing. His words, however, are true but his intentions were out of line and foolish. While living in the city of Chicago Toomer turned the heads of many colleagues when they noticed his appearance in the big city. A close friend of Toomer wrote to her husband, "It seems that in Chicago they do not know that he has Negro blood-he seems to claim French extraction" (Byrd & Gates Jr.). At that time Chicago had many black musicians, artists, and overall entertainers coming from the area. Those words made it seem like Toomer was not fond of the image of being labeled as one of the many black artists in the Chicago area. Cane is the collection that Toomer wrote and is still a popular reading that many enjoy today. The problem that Toomer faced after the collection was if he was another image of the New Negro Movement or the Lost Generation (black people passing off as white)?

Jean Toomer was raised by his grandparents and mother, as his father abandoned him. He was dealt a large amount of knowledge about his Negro heritage and many other cultures that lived within his body. Toomer did not believe in labeling himself for the public eye unless it was to his advantage. In his childhood, he was raised as a mulatto elite member, meaning he was a part of both black and white societies. He went to schools that were predominantly black or white. As he grew into a young adult, he would categorize himself as an American and throw away from the label of being a black or white American. "Bona and Paul," is one of the first short stories that Toomer wrote, and the theme surrounds the idea of passing off as white. The theme did not sit well with many blacks because they felt as though Toomer was ashamed of his blackness and that identifying himself as white would be an advantage and make things easier while living in America.

Toomer did go on to marry twice and both women were white. That is not an insult toward Toomer because I believe love is love and color is not a factor when finding your true love. Toomer did have to suffer the same as any other minority that married outside of their race. Toomer may have passed off enough to live in white neighborhoods but marrying a white woman during the 1940s was very dangerous for him to do. His uncle did not agree with Toomer denounced his African heritage and believed that his mother and grandparents would be gravely upset to see him disregard his roots. Toomer even went as far as to say that he never lived as a Negro. With all the trials and tribulations that his ancestors and black people were facing at the time that statement is as disrespectful as O.J. Simpson saying, "I'm not black, I'm OJ."

Rexroth states that Toomer was the first poet to successfully combine folk and elite culture in his writings. That may be true when speaking of his poetry, but this is another example of Toomer taking advantage of a culture he doesn't love. Toomer did not only denounce his blackness, but he rode the train of folk culture in his writing. "Reapers," is a poem written by Toomer in 1923 and the theme is about the job of a reaper, a person or machine that harvests a crop. This may not be exciting to the reader, but his violent visuals speak to the men of this job. This poem is from *The Norton Anthology of Modern and Contemporary Poetry*.

> Black reapers with the sound of steel on stones
> Are sharpening scythes. I see them place the hones
> In their hip-pockets as a thing that's done,
> And start their silent swinging, one by one.
> Black horses drive a mower through the weeds,
> And there, a field rat, startled, squealing bleeds.
> His belly close to ground. I see the blade,
> Blood-stained, continue cutting weeds and shade.

The image of a black reaper working this type of job and not being able to fully understand the words that are being said by Toomer on the page is very ironic. The audience is sickened by the work of these men that have killed this field rat and how they would still eat the crop that once had the stained blood of this rat. The white elite would read this as filth and be grateful that they do not have to work such nasty jobs while the folk people are not very fond of the nasty picture that Toomer paof ints the hard work they do with those crops.

Toomer was married to writer Margery Latimer and after her death, he married Marjorie Content was the daughter of a Jewish stockbroker. Being married to a white woman in that society may have been difficult for Toomer to live through because of all the racism. "Portrait in Georgia," is a poem that he wrote to give his idea of how the South felt about interracial marriage at the time.

> Hair--braided chestnut,
> coiled like a lyncher's rope,
> Eyes--fagots,
> Lips--old scars, or the first red blisters,
> Breath--the last sweet scent of cane,
> And her slim body, white as the ash
>
> of black flesh after flame.

This poem gives great imagery by comparing a white woman to the lynching of a black man. "The last sweet scent of cane," line references his great collection Cane, but after that was published Toomer began to claim himself as a white man. The reader could see this as Toomer saying that a white woman could be damaging to a black man, but he was married to two white women. This further proves his identity crisis of not understanding whether he can understand the African American experience. For him, this may be a portrait, but it is in fact a harsh reality that many black men had to deal with lynchings in America. For Toomer to take something so disturbing and turn it into a symbol of the taboo of his love for white women was very odd and the reader may see it in a different light, but the black community was probably not fond of having such a sickening crime be sexualized by his words.

Kenneth Rexroth is a great writer on his own, but he was inaccurate when he stated that Jean Toomer was both the most important black poet and successively combined both the folk and elite cultures in his writing. The reasoning behind the stance is that Toomer did not identify himself as a black man, so he could not be seen as the most important African American writer and he was the ultimate opportunist. He took advantage of his opportunities whether it was for the good or bad of society, he will be remembered as a great writer that can help many young people today who have their own identity crises or feel as though they are not accepted in their own community. His writings are still controversial pieces that can help spark a debate and his imagery is great for writers to read and learn from. Marcus Garvey once said, "The Black skin is not a badge of shame, but rather a glorious symbol of national greatness." Many black writers have written many pieces and this quote sticks with me after reading their pieces, but Toomer did not feel the same as Garvey and many other black writers and that is why I feel that he is not, as Rexroth states, the most important black poet.

---

*The works cited are on the acknowledgments page.

I Am the Night, Color Me Black

The Vampiric Positionality of the Black Pedagogue in Ganja & Hess

by FALLEN MATTHEWS

Historians surmise that Blaxploitation saved what was, in hindsight, a self-destructive film industry. Hollywood neared bankruptcy as production, marketing, and distribution costs exceeded revenue in the 1970s (Lykidis 16). Movies made little if any profits in the scheme of extravagant sets, stars, and styles that underperformed commercially. Cinema viewership declined in the wake of a residential shift to the suburbs, far from the inner cities where theatres were based (Saucier 454). Unsparing budgets and white celebrities underscored the luxuriant narratives of Classical Hollywood and New Hollywood, a standard of life onscreen that was inimical to the cultures and politics offscreen which arose from the waste lain by World War II, Cold War tensions, and the outset of the Vietnam War (Lawrence 17). However, blaxploitation monetized African American audiences, a viewership once dismissed to be fiscally negligible although they comprised roughly 30 percent of moviegoers (12). They found a reprieve in antiheroes and vigilantes, embodiments of resistance to the white hegemony whose definitive requisite was the systemic anti-Blackness Civil Rights and Black Nationalist movements opposed (Guerrero 3, 8). Melvin Van Peebles' Sweet Sweetback's Badaaass Song, whose confident and cunning protagonist challenges and bests jurisdictive anti-Blackness, is most widely cited as the film that catalyzed the Blaxploitation genre (11). Gordon Parks Jr.'s Superfly further modeled Blaxploitation as a lucrative venture whose film and soundtrack generated a vast profit (Quinn 99). Lower production costs engendered cinematic realism: a visuality that endowed films with greater fidelity to real life affected in scene, setting, and storyline-location respective to narrative milieux. Against their modest budgets in the thousands, these films grossed millions.

While Blaxploitation may use elements from other genres like fantasy, horror, noir, and westerns; Blaxploitation generically is characterized by the portrayal of Black everyday people who incisively, contentiously overcome anti-Blackness (Terry 85). Bill Gunn's experimental Ganja & Hess does this uniquely as the film depicts an Afrocentric discursive conquest. The film follows Dr. Hess Green (Duane Jones), an anthropologist who becomes a vampire after his intellectual albeit erratic and suicidal assistant, George (Bill Gunn), impales him with an accursed dagger. The doctor falls in love with his assistant's widow, Ganja (Marlene Clark), who resolves to become likewise once she discovers Hess' vampiric nature. Vampirism takes on a new meaning with realism and racialization as African American positionalities continue to be afflicted by disparity, exploitation, exclusion, and inaccessibility alongside systematic anti-Blackness which extenuates our adversities. I find myself immortalized by pearls of wisdom that speak to ancestral strength and blood memory, akin to how kernels from an artifact—the cursed dagger—transform Dr. Hess Green and Ganja Meda into the undead.

In his suicide note, George opines on the inexorable perils and traumas that scourge African Americans in academia. He encourages Black academics to distrust the intellectualism and educational systems as they were cultivated through and rife with Eurocentrism. "Philosophy is a prison," he says, "It disregards the uncustomary things about you. The result of individual thought is accruable only to itself." For me, this is nascent of recent equality, diversity, inclusion, and accessibility (EDIA) initiatives which actually underscore the academe's proclivity to hegemonize: commodify the very sanctions which impact scant as is marginalized peoples, to graft and implement repatriation and reparation in its own image. Gainfully employed academics are able to exercise power that is epistemically inaccessible. They glean assets from the ubiquity of a colonialist meritocracy which posits the expenditure and function of education as wholesome, a conclusive paradigm for innovation with little, if any iniquitous purpose. I know this to be untrue. Therein, I often find myself at a loss as the sole Black and First Nations

[Afro-L'nu] non-binary [demigirl] person amidst gainfully employed and other privileged positionalities who 'champion' EDIA whilst their professional and discursive sanctums are buttressed by and contingent upon disparities. When my people remain absent, when nothing is done to amend the 'precarity' through which their absence is sustained, it is not enough to merely acknowledge or concede that the institution is woefully lacking. EDIA avows itself as a sliding door: the aperture suspended from a grand track, operant upon multitudes rather than dichotomous hinges; the rectifier that equalizes ostensibly negligible aspects that make or break what matters most. The reality for BIPOC has been, is, and remains as revolving doors: partitions turn about a colonial axis—methodologies, theories, praxes, erasures—where disparities (the very ones that EDIA claims to amend) recur continuously wherein marginalized peoples come and go but are unable to stay.

The more I critically consider my positionality and academic exegesis, the more I realize that vampirism underlays my transformation, survival, and demise as graduation is fated as expulsion. I grow increasingly desensitized to praise and more aware of how praise—or acknowledgment—does nothing to ensure my professorship, some semblance of financial security, or palpable prestige. EDIA itself is vampiric in its avid solicitation of insights and labor from the very marginalized positionalities it purports to uplift. The wealth of lip service paid in comparison to what pittances we marginalized peoples are afforded is abysmal. The voices of Black and Indigenous positionalities are always in demand, but not our well-being. George speaks to this, noting the Eurocentric affinity to supplant essence with performativity: "Gesture destroys concept. Involvement mortifies vanity... To be adored...is to be a symbol of success, and you must not succeed on any terms..." He tells us, "You are the despised of the earth," a reference to Franz Fanon's The Wretched of the Earth (also translatable to The Damned of the Earth; French: Les Damnés de la Terre) whose title itself harks from Jacques Roumain's Sales Nègres, a poem that laments on the struggles of "dirty niggers" as a colonized populace amongst other subjugated peoples: "And there we stand, all the damned of the earth" (Aksan).

There is an existential quandary posed by my academic prowess, knowing that catharsis entails addressing—not merely acknowledging—the ways in which colonialism, capitalism, and hegemony have affected my ability to relate to others. The objectification inherent to academic institutions proffers that everything and everyone can be possessed, in addition to the material—medaled—representations of intellect and altruism. It is hard to discern between one's calling to learn or educate and one's desire to accumulate so that one may optimize their material or occupational acquisition. People qualitatively bleed me dry—take, take, take. Conversely, I am encouraged to siphon—whenever, wherever, whomever, however possible—within and beyond reach and revel in what I have wrought. Death holds no bearing as extraction persists even when one ceases to live. The academe will simply assimilate our mortality into its metrics because it is only able to memorialize us respective to the accreditation failure or success, in the scheme of our ancestors, peers, or successors. Whereas our demise further augments our own anguish as we become desiccate and strive to draw, from whatever so that we might fulfill our hallows. Ganja & Hess depicts this as we, Black peoples, stand to become monstrous as infections and emulators of a hegemonic—in particular, the academic colonialist—enterprise.

Blaxploitation spawns vampirism as a vehicle to explore the coalescence of need and desire in hunger. I reflect on how those privileged positionalities who allege to admire me are the same who dispirit the slightest inclination that they advocate for more, if not for me than for others who make fill the hallows they so earnestly acknowledge; the same who disaffect my fears and ambitions so as to blaspheme any actant as gluttony whereas silence is temperance.

---

*The works cited are on the acknowledgments page.

Right To Be Black

by Chris "The Poetic Genius" Green

They taught me my black skin was a sin
Until it singed in my psyche not to like me
I looked in the mirror thought it was too dark
Thought I would like a light me
They taught me my people only had history in chains
Whipped into my mind I was once inferior
Until it scarred my interior
Only showed me Roots not my roots
I just knew...
It had to be more
Didn't know we had kings and queens before
Crafted science and mathematics
Maybe I could've believed I was meant to grasp it
But the only thing I saw subtracted were rights
Like a right to justice and peace
Get killed holding Skittles and tea
Trying to taste rainbows and embrace sunshine
Told me I was the darkness
But I dance to the beat of my God's love
Light on my feet
Fist in the air
Knowing no matter how the odds are stacked...
I have a right to be black
That the hue of my human is beautiful
That my life has value and meaning above the demeaning
So, you can stamp on me colored like we all aren't

If you must
Truth is we're all dust
And I'm proud of my strand
And I'll stand
Head held high and back straight
And the whip of your tongue can't bend it
Cause my spirit meant it when it said it loud
"I'm black and I'm proud!"

I'M BLACK AND I'M PROUD!

Love yourself no matter the color
But more importantly, love each other

Whole Numbers

by Stephani Maari Booker

We don't count,
we ain't never counted.
We couldn't count,
wasn't allowed to learn
to read no numbers.
We wasn't supposed
to be nothin'
never was nothin'
never be nothin',
remember?

Nah! Remember this:
We were always somthin',
we wasn't never zero.
We counted when
they wanted to add.
Slave states multiplying
to get more votes
more representatives
more wealth.
But they subtracted,
made each of us
three-fifths human,
dividing to conquer.

We were products,
denominated as
quotients with
differences,
but they used
our quantities,
our multitudes of
hidden figures.

Time to seize the
strength of our sums.
We are greater than,
never less than,
and always equal.
Show our totals
in the streets
on the rolls
and at the polls.
We ain't fractions—
that old math is incorrect.
We are whole numbers
to the Infinite Power.

but when I was 4 the world seemed fine

after Geoffrey Canada

BY NEFERTITI ASANTI

in the orange room. with the wooden box. the prize box there
is x-men trading cards. i choose mystique. she is a mutant. her
blue skin. her choice. in the cartoons i watch with my big sister,
mystique becomes whoever she wants to be. she is a villain. she
is a bad girl. she is a mutant. in the orange room. in the wooden
box. the prize box. i choose the villain. i choose her blue skin.
the prize box doesn't have a lot of girl choices. no storm. no jubilee.
no rogue. i choose the villain. i choose the bad girl mutant. she
chooses her own skin. i wonder what it is like to choose the skin
you're in. like let's say i was born blue & mutant. would that make
me a bad girl? would i still be a black girl? would i have super
powers? would i be allowed to stay here? in the orange room with
the wooden box. the prize box. if i answered the questions good,
say a square has 4 sides, a triangle has 3, & a triangle on top
of a square is a house. & the owl goes hoo. & the cow goes moo.
if i get all the answers right, would they let me have the whole prize
box? would they let me stay here? or would they disappear me
to a special school for mutant kids that are smart enough to be evil?

kids in my class disappear all the time. are they mutants? are they
really blue on the inside? i ask mommy if my classmates that are no
longer in class if they are mutants & mommy says no they are
immigrants who came from a far away place for a better life but

their family didn't get permission, like when you get a hall pass to go
to the bathroom or when mommy signs the letter that says it's ok
for miss andrea & miss carol to take me to the zoo with the rest
of the school. i ask mommy what's so hard about getting permission.
mommy says it's complicated & i know it means she don't wanna talk
no more.

in the orange room. with the wooden box. the prize box. if i answer all
the questions good i wish i could win superpowers. i wish i could wish
princesa, nadira & josef back & we could take turns choosing & changing
skin & it wouldn't matter if we were mutants or immigrants or children
of mystique cuz we'd all be friends in the orange room with the wooden
box the prize box sitting between us.

Statistical Iconoclast

by Richard May III

Room Crowded with Crusty noses
& Pink Eye Curiosity welcomed
Me-
today's art teacher in my son's class
Crayon conversations on paper mimicked
Umizoomi sketch smiles
Sponge Bob frowns

Memory moon-walked
I am a father who is the son of two fathers
The son of two men who loved my mother
Biology of one man birthed my voice
Another man's scaffolding water-colored my hands
Legacy of both men mentored
Re-appearance of Ellison's *Invisible man*
no longer disappearing
shattering Wright's *Bigger Thomas* statistic seeping
circus mirror reflection

Now- Hero to my son
His *Batman Superman Spiderman*
& Dad

painting elementary memories for a father-famished generation

Acknowledgment

by Richard May III

My Giant Steps
Tenor Sax
through classroom maze
Door blows open
Teacher shouts
"Hocus Pocus!"
Tattle-tellers respond
"Everybody Focus!"
Teacher secretly tells fatherless tales to me
Of little ones starving for Papa affection
Says "You are the only Dad who visits"
Index nose picker fingers point
Father-famished eyes gaze wishfully
21st-century man-child remix of my me
whispers to table neighbor with Lion King pride
"That's my Dad!"

1st Place Winner

BY RICHARD MAY III

See Jesse Owens
Disguised as 9-remix-me
Glide in Victory

Driven to Manhood

BY RICHARD MAY III

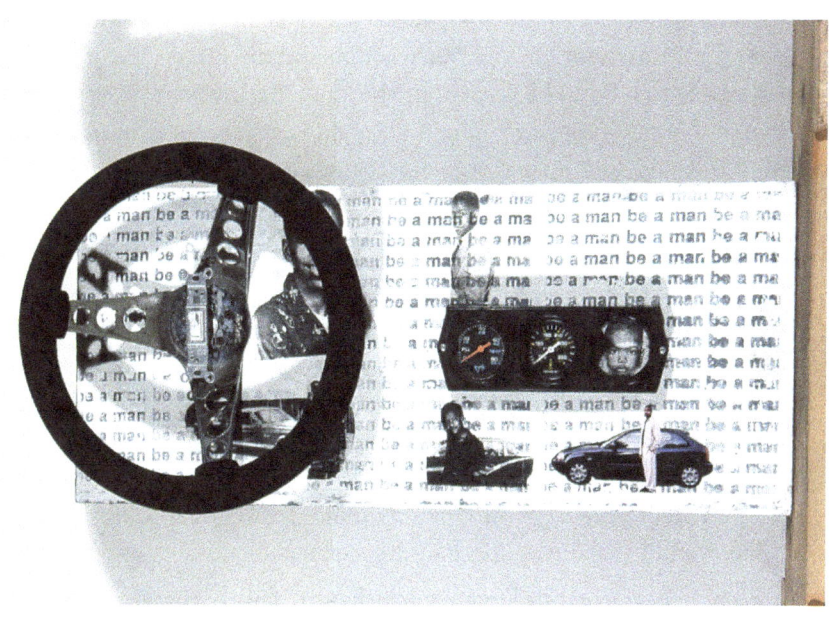

I Guess I *Am* Invisible, and That Matters

BY DENISE T. BEST

Racism. As a person of Bajan-American descent growing up in Boston, you became familiar with the concept at an early age, but you could never get used to it, to *passively* accept it. What you did was adjust the manner in which you dealt with it on a daily basis, depending on the who, what, when, where, how, and sometimes why. It mattered. I mean, what could you *do*, or say *to* Sister Padua, your 6th-grade nun, when she called your friend a nigger? Not much, but my reaction mattered. I told my mother, and her reaction surprised me. Her full lips grimaced into a straight line when she said, "If anyone ever calls you a nigger, I want you to get up and get your coat; do not wait until the end of the day! Get up and get your coat and come home immediately and tell me.

Whoa! That was unbelievably radical for my even-tempered mother, I mean she rarely even yelled at me and my two younger siblings. My sister and I still laugh about the time she yelled at us to quiet down so she could hear her soap, *Love is Life*. "Did you hear what I said, I said?", she said. We laughed so hard about it that we made her laugh. But racism was no laughing matter to her, and I waited with bated breath for one of those racist Catholics to call me a nigger, mostly because I was dying to know what my mother was going to do, but the obedient child that I was, that never happened.

I never kept count, but I'm guessing that my family experienced hundreds of occurrences of just out-and-out, in-your-face racism, often recognizably lurking behind Colgate smiles, in the intervening years between sixth grade and applying to Lesley College. I had always known that I wanted to be a teacher. It was a tough decision between attending Spellman, where I longed to belong and enrolling in the best teacher's college in the country, which completed the Harvard/

Radcliffe/Lesley triangle, where I didn't and did not *want* to belong.

The application process required applicants to affix a passport photo to the tiny square in the upper right-hand corner of the front of the application. I almost missed the deadline agonizing as to whether to glue my photo to that application or not. There was a strong possibility that if the wrong person reviewed my file, I would be rejected despite my transcript and SAT scores. On the other hand, would they reject me because I didn't follow the instructions and my application was technically incomplete? I prayed to the God of the Catholics, who up to that point had never answered any of my prayers, and sent in my application sans photo. I prayed that it really wouldn't matter.

Imagine my surprise when at the Dean's Tea, held during the first week of classes, I raised my hand in response to a question, and she called me by name, "Denise?" I looked to my right, left, and then behind me, certain that she was calling on some other Denise, as I had never seen her before in my life, and I had *not* included a photo with my application. "Aah, the process of elimination!", I mused. As one of only nine Black freshmen, I suspected that I was the *only* one who had *not* submitted a photo. She apparently had committed everyone else's visage to memory. As a matter of fact, my intentional invisibility had outed me.

By my sophomore year at Lesley University, I was the co-chair of the Black Student Union and had already found our first African American professor. We had a Nigerian economics professor who made my ears bleed; I mean, I didn't know what he was saying, and I didn't know what the hell he was talking about either. When I asked Dean Ritvo why there was a distinct lack of Black professors, she said they couldn't find any. I don't remember how, and it really doesn't matter, but I sure found one, and that was how I dealt with that! Betty Moore was hired to teach sociology, and she was there long enough to receive tenure as well.

It was the following year that my Developmental Math professor, who taught us how to teach math, refused to call on the only Black student in his class. I am not exaggerating. If I was the only one with my hand raised, braced by my left hand at the elbow as I had grown tired of waving it, he would literally answer the question himself. One day, about a month into that racist practice, and fully fortified having read Sam Greenlee's book, *The Spook Who Sat by the Door*, I slammed my textbook shut as loud as humanely possible, scraped my chair back, stood up and announced, "Well, I guess I *am* Invisible!" I stomped my way to the classroom door, exited, and slammed the door behind me. Yeah, what I did was adjust the manner in which I dealt with racism daily, depending on the who, what, when, where, how, and sometimes why. It matters.

In May of 1975, I graduated from Lesley University near the top of my class, but not with honors. I just missed Cum Laude due to the incredible number of "B" pluses and "A" minuses on my transcript. Not one "A" was granted, not even from Prof. Sheila Clark, whose suburban classroom I visited at her request. She had observed me teaching after which she asked me to demonstrate how to incorporate creative moments in her academic classes. No extra credit, or cash for that "off the books" mini-course, that none of my Caucasian counterparts had offered, just the condescending "A-", for her course in Learning Disabilities.

Luckily for me, throughout my bigoted, educational experiences, my mother repeatedly stated, "Just pay attention; they can't take your knowledge from you." I found out she had been right. I finished out the school year as a permanent sub in the elementary school where I had done my student teaching, and I picked it back up in September. I got to teach nearly every day until that December, when I finally got assigned my own third-grade classroom, at the James Hennigan School in Jamaica Plain, MA.

When the main office secretary made the introductions, the principal, Mr. Prendergast, barely shook my hand. His fingers sort of fluttered next to the palm of my right hand. That was a first. I was offended, that shit mattered! I later learned that he had not wanted another Black teacher in *his* school. I was the third Black teacher of a teaching staff of 53!

Every morning, Mr. Prendergast positioned himself at the top of the first landing, parting the swarm of teachers and pupils to the left or right of him like some malevolent dictator. On my first day, as I passed him to the right, I disingenuously proclaimed, "Good morning", to no response. I guess he didn't see me", I thought to myself. On day two, the same thing. "Good morning.", I said as if butter wouldn't melt in my mouth. No response. Maybe he didn't hear me over the cacophony of voices. I decided to say good morning to that son of a bitch one more time. Day three, yup, nope... that was it! That was the day *he* became invisible *to me.*

I proudly proclaim that I am a damn good teacher. In my first year of teaching, I brought the reading level of each kid in my class up one whole grade. The vice principal privately complimented me and publicly rewarded my kids for the way that they orderly, yet casually walked in pairs to the cafeteria on the lower level, while the rest of the kids burst out of the classroom doors of disinterested keepers and ran down the stairs as if access to food was limited.

One day, I walked into my classroom after lunch to find Prendergast standing at my desk paging through my lesson plan book. Perhaps he had never seen one before. I certainly hadn't seen one on any desk of the mostly Boston State graduates. He moved away from my desk as I entered. He never said a word, just nodded his begrudging approval as he walked by me and out the door. I was surprised that the sense of satisfaction truly mattered to me.

During my third year, and before my tenure, due to the aftermath of a teacher's strike, I got bumped out of my position. I was astounded when Prendergast offered me an opportunity to teach basic ed and GED in an adult ed center, where he knew the director personally. Apparently, somewhere along the line, I had gained visibility. I mattered!

Adhering to my mother's wise advice, "Be a good listener and keep your mouth shut.", I quickly learned that the small, full-time staff at The Adult Center of Education consisted of a mother/daughter, an aunt/niece combo, friends, and me. There was also a Chinese woman named Edie, who taught part-time in the afternoons. I was the only full-time teacher who did not have a key to the Center, which was located on the third floor of a downtown office building on Franklin Street in Boston. The Kneeland Street bus dropped me off at about 8:30, so every morning I had to wait out in the hall until someone arrived at 9:00 with a key. I thought of making an argument for a key, but having learned to pick my battles, I decided that the manner in which to deal with this act of passive-aggressive racism was to simply ignore it.

Just before my wedding and relocation to Connecticut, someone broke into the school and stole several GED exam booklets, invalidating every GED exam in the nation. That bit of news was shared with me at the same moment that I was informed that the feds were in attendance, and I needed to join the rest of the staff up front. They were all lined up facing the four grim-looking federal agents, side by side, all of *them* looking absolutely petrified. We were told that there was no evidence of a forced entry, so someone must have had a key.

I remember how I very dramatically looked down the line to my left, and into every face on my right and pronounced, "Well, I'm the only one here without a key, sooo, I'll be leaving!" And just like that I walked out unrestrained and quickly made my way down the stairs and out into the throng of downtown pedestrians, and because we all look alike, I easily made myself invisible. Sometimes, just sometimes, when it really matters, you could adjust the manner in which you dealt with daily acts of racism, and depending on the who, what, when, where, how, and sometimes why, you could use their own racism against them.

The breath of Black men is precious

by Dion Jahmal

Inspired by "Those who need a true story." by Tara Betts

They will attempt to treat him like a boy all his life. That's why I call him man. He calls his son over to him. Young Jahmal approaches, he gently places his thick hands on the little man's tiny shoulders. Daddy shapes small clay hands into fists and holds them in front of Jahmals face. Puts manchild in the proper stance.

Left foot slightly in front of right... toe in line with heel... tuck chin.

Jahmal describes the tete-a-tete as the breath of fresh air needed to resuscitate a young man, giving him the life needed in a world turned anhedonic.

The sweet science echoes in the psyche of this young warrior, his father's voice wrapped in knowledge and tied tight with the twine of agape.

Hands up, chin tucked slightly, protect yourself at all times....

His presence is a present, fountains of chocolate insight poured into a young chalis eager to drink. There is empathy in the requests of the father.

Hands up, chin tucked slightly, protect yourself at all times....

He mimics the footwork and punches thrown from the battered warrior, whose crisp punches and slick pivots reflect the footwork needed in the squared circle of black reality. Jahmal wanted to stop punching, but daddy needed to save his life.

Hands up, chin tucked, protect yourself at all times...

After his last punch was thrown, Jahmal looked at his father who was still throwing punches.

Enough punches for his fathers tortured childhood.

Enough punches for trees bearing bodies on their limbs.

Enough punches for being told he'd be nothing but a janitor, and it becomes true.

The constant fight to live one more day follows melanated flesh like a sun of despair, poisoned air rots them from the inside out as they scratch for crumbs.
The children should live soft lives wrapped in rainbows of redemption and never tell the story of ghetto life until fathers teach them to throw punches.

Hands up, chin tucked, protect yourself at all times....

The Sweet Science

by Karen Frederick

Boys were lined up outside at 7:00 a.m. on Saturday. It was autumn they were in the midst of Indian summer, and it was warm and sunny. Even the air had a golden glow. It had rained overnight, and the streets were washed clean. Most of the boys walked to the club but some had come from far northeast on the bus. Thirty boys of all shapes and sizes stood outside waiting for Mr. Walter to open up. Mr. Walter was out back with a half-chewed cigar in his mouth and a beat-up-looking Bowery Boys hat on his head cleaning up the alley. He was sweeping up bottles and trash and the left-over dreams of Friday night. He used to believe the sweet taste of bourbon, cherries, sugar, and ice would not become the sour taste of regret the next day. Now he knew better. Mr. Walter had given up the bottle some years back and was now a church-going man. He went to church 'most every night of the week except Friday night. Friday night and Saturday he shared his devotion to God and worshipped at the altar of the sweet science.

Mr. Walter had boxed AAU in Detroit and had never lost his love for the game. He always arrived first to sweep up the alley and mop the concrete floor inside. He unlocked the back door and began to work using the industrial-strength bleach and cleanser he brought from his janitor's job at Freedman's Hospital. It was a hard job but a good job "for a man done been to jail" his wife said.

Inside the main room there was a small area of several thick mats covered in canvas and surrounded by four metal posts screwed into the floor. The canvas was stretched tight so that the floor of the ring had some give when you stepped on it. There was a big globe light that hung overhead and two buckets, one at each corner. There was a heavy bag, two-speed bags, and several jump ropes hung on pegs on the walls. There was a big picture of Sugar Ray Robinson, cut from the newspaper and glued to the wall.

James T. and his friend Reggie had walked the twenty blocks from

Georgia Avenue. James T. pressed his nose against the glass door to see if anyone was around. He shifted his weight from one foot to the other.

What's the matter with you? Reggie asked.

"I gotta...." James T.. replied.

"Gotta what?"

"Gotta go." James T.. replied quietly.

"Well, knock then."

Reggie looked at the other boys waiting in line and pushed James T. towards the door.

James T. swallowed hard. Everyone knew the club never opened before 7:30 but they always lined up by 7:00 a.m. Many of the boys came by bus from far northeast and if they missed the early bus they wouldn't get to the club until 8:00. James T. knew that Mr. Walter didn't like to be disturbed while he was working.

James T. knocked loudly.

Mr. Walter moved his cigar from the right side of his mouth to the left side and bit down as he went to the front door. Sunshine was streaming in and he could not see who was knocking.

"Cut out that racket." He yelled. "I'm comin'"

He unlocked the top lock and the bottom lock, turned the deadbolt, took off the chain, and opened the door a crack. He looked around and didn't see anybody until he looked down at a small figure with a big head on a very small boy.

"I gotta go – to the toilet."

James T. followed Mr. Walter into the club and he heard the metal door slam shut. He'd been so nervous waiting outside. But now, following Mr. Walter, he felt something stirring in his chest like a small butterfly hovering over honeysuckle. He went to the bathroom while Mr. Walter finished sweeping up the office. He shook himself off and wiped his hands on the back of his pants. He ran past Mr. Walter to the front door.

"Boy come back here,"

James T. swallowed. "Sir."

"What's your name, boy?"

"James T..."

"Well, Mr. James T. there's no wet paper towels in this trashcan. Did you wash yo' hands?"

"Yes sir." James T. replied.

"Why didn't you dry them?"

James T. didn't want to admit that he was too short to reach the paper towels.

"It dries when you go outside." James T.. said. He turned to go back outside to the line of boys waiting outside.

"Mr. James T.., you ate?"

James T. looked around wondering if Mr. Walter was really talking to him.

"No suh" he replied.

"Come here boy." Mr. Walter turned over a crate and motioned for James T. to sit. Mr. Walter took his big metal lunchbox that looked like a mailbox and sat it on a crate between the two of them. Inside there were two big sandwiches, an apple, a slice of cake, and a thermos.

"This yo first day?" Mr. Walter went over to the bathroom to wash his hands and came back and sat down.

"Yes suh." James T. could smell the good smells coming from the lunchbox.

Mr. Walter opened one of the sandwiches and gave James T. half. It was still steaming hot and wrapped in thick white paper with a string that said Red Rose Café. It was a bacon egg and cheese sandwich on toasted white bread. James T. picked up the half sandwich with both hands and took a big bite out of the middle getting a piece of egg all over his face.

James T. was hungry and took a second bite and wiped his hands on the paper napkin. He looked around and breathed in the place. The neatly hung dingy towels, the boxes for lockers, the sweat-stained concrete floor. He heard the echo of the speed bag ground into the walls.

They ate for a while in silence.

Mr. Walter, you think I could learn to box?" James T. watched the side of Mr. Walter's face as he chewed.

"Nothin' a man cain't learn if he's willing to pay the price."

James T. thought about this for a while and finished chewing his sandwich. Mr. Walter opened his thermos and poured an inch of coffee into the small cup for James T. and two inches in the big cup for himself. The coffee had condensed milk and brown sugar and was hot and good. They sat and drank coffee and chewed their sandwich and thought about the day ahead.

A Day with QueenE

by GLORIA SMITH

(as told to Michael G. Hickey)

In the Fall of 1967, Nashville, TN, nine-year-old Gloria was nearly inseparable from her older cousin, Eddie, but there was one day in particular that would stay permanently chiseled in her memory like cut granite.

"I was a shy little black girl in fifth grade who adored my crazy gay cousin, Eddie," Gloria said. "My mother was a pianist who traveled all over the country, and my daddy was an Army medic in someplace called 'Vietnam,' so Eddie was my role model."

Gloria would have done anything for Eddie. The perfect cocktail of unapologetic, flamboyant, and ostentatious, Eddie was every bit of his true self with an extra dash or two thrown in for good keeping. Gloria's sister called him "QueenE" with a capital "E" – all one word. Eddie was a black Freddie Mercury before Freddie Mercury. He danced ballet and had the most perfectly lithe male body Gloria had ever seen. He was tall – over six feet, and every muscle was braided into every other muscle like steel cables. He also attended Fisk University where he was majoring in, apparently… pretty much everything. (Eddie was a fourth-year sophomore.)

"Psst, hey skinny brown girl, y'all up? We gotta big day today." Eddie peeked inside Gloria's bedroom on a Saturday morning, just like a million other Saturday mornings, another opportunity for Gloria to tag along with "The Fabulous QueenE" or, as he preferred to be addressed: *his Royal High-Ass.*

"Eddie was always teasing me about something," she said. "He was so funny, but he also had his serious side. Each day in his Royal Court, in his Royal presence, I was instructed to *catch a life lesson.*"

Because her young brain struggled to keep up with all the rules of the Royal Court, Gloria was constantly reminded that the first commandment of QueenE was *Thou Shalt Kneel*. "Even if," he would add, "it's just a polite bow with the eyes lowered. This is to be always observed, should you be in the presence of the Lord, an Elder, or QueenE, baby girl! Kings come and go – always running off to shoot someone or beat on some war drum. Whereas a Queen stays next to the nectar, close to the hive. QueenE prefers life on the sweet and sunny side." Then he would snap his fingers four times in the form of a Z.

Eddie talked like this all the time, even in the morning when Gloria was still asleep and he was softly whispering in her ear. She knew the kneeling thing was really about praying to God 'cause, "Eddie did it all the time and always said the Lord Almighty was more likely to hear your prayers if you were on your knees at the throne."

Gloria wondered if that part about the "sweet and sunny side" was why her grandmum called her 'Honey" and "Sweetie." Eddie and grandmum were always hugging each other and sometimes would simultaneously say, "Be kind. Always." Then after that, they would say, "Those are two separate sentences." Then they would laugh and hug even harder.

Gloria's grandmum had something called "black girl magic" and so did Eddie. She was the only person Eddie ever backed down from. One day, Eddie was gay-splaining his philosophy of how to be happy. The day before, he had died his Afro platinum blond. He was wearing pink short-shorts and a sky-blue tank-top. His muscles rippled all over the map.

"Most worker bees stay in some sort of brain-controlled formation," he would say between sips of chamomile tea. "No one out of line. It gets even worse for some worker bees as life keeps moving and moving until one day, the worker bees walking behind you start to walk on top of you. They want to keep you in line. They want your 'hive brain' in proper working condition in order to control you and the other worker bees, to trap you deep in the hive forever."

Gloria got dressed in her culottes and pigtails then Cousin Eddie ushered her out the door. They were off to meet Eddie's gay frat brothers from Fisk, and then they were going to a very special lunch with a very special guest. "For me," Gloria said, "Eddie was the Queen Bee, and the rest of the world was his colony. We all loved QueenE." One day, he taught Gloria the top ten rules on how to be a girl:"

1.) Don't be afraid to cry.

2.) Never let anyone see you cry.

3.) Don't kiss a boy unless you really like him.

4.) Wear as much makeup as you damn well please except at church.

5.) Get involved in politics. Don't let other people make all your decisions.

6.) Always tell the truth, not just when it's convenient.

7.) Always do what's right even if no one's watching because God don't blink.

8.). Use your greatest asset - your eyes. They are not just a window to your soul, they are a reflection of it. Use your eyes to show your heart, to show your 'never-give-in' and 'never-give-up.'

9.) When you see a puppy, a kitty, or a baby bird, speak very softly so you don't scare it.

10.) The "weaker sex" is actually the stronger sex, and don't let anyone tell you differently. A woman gives birth. There's nothing more powerful than that. Women start lives. Men start wars.

"Snap to it my royal subjects. Fall in formation." Eddie said as he and Gloria and all the frat brothers piled into the van and left for the special lunch.

*   *   *   *   *

"Earlier that summer," Gloria said, "I was playing jump rope with my best friend Karen. She lived right across the street, and we played all day until the streetlights came on. Then, if we didn't come inside, Eddie or grandmum would open the screen door and announce to the entire neighborhood, "Dinnertime, girl. Getcha booty in here!"

One night, Karen asked if they could play a little longer, but Gloria could see grandmum standing hands-on-hips at the screen door. "Sorry," Gloria said.

The next day, Gloria found out that a man in a big truck had hit Karen as she was walking home. Her 18-inch ponytail got tangled in the rear axle, and the driver dragged her under his truck for three blocks. Witnesses reported he then got out in the middle of the road, dumped her dead body on the curb, and drove off. He was never arrested.

"That's when Eddie really started to come around for me," Gloria said. "I didn't talk to anyone for weeks," Gloria said. "Not a single word. And I cried every day. He knew I was a sensitive girl. Eddie knew all about sensitive girls. I figured that's why he was taking me to this lunch with his friends."

They all squeezed out of the van and into The Krystal lunch counter on Fifth Avenue in downtown Nashville. There was a sign in the window that read WHITE ONLY, but Eddie and his friends didn't care about that. They weren't there to eat. They all went inside and sat, and sat, and sat some more. No one took their order. Every time someone came into the diner, a bell rang, and if they were black, they were ignored. Then suddenly, the bell rang and everyone immediately stopped talking. Heads swiveled in unison. Chairs scooted back. There was a hushed silence. People, black and white, simultaneously rose to their feet. It was the quietest moment Gloria had ever experienced, even quieter than the church.

In walked six black men wearing dark overcoats and in the middle of them, as if being protected by the rest of the herd, was another black man in a fedora and long white pea coat. His name was Martin Luther King Jr. "I had never heard of him," Gloria said, "but Eddie and his friends sure had. They stared in awe as if Dr. King was some fantastic star shooting across the galaxy."

It would be several years until Gloria completely understood the significance of that day. "I loved and worshipped Cousin Eddie the same way he loved and worshipped Martin," she said.

Less than a year later, when King was assassinated on April 4, 1968, Gloria watched Eddie cry as she had never seen a grown-up cry before. He watched the TV and wept with a pillow up to his face, muffling the wailing. Then he began moaning a pained mantra over and over, "No, no, please God, no, don't let it be him. Please God, please no…" Gloria gave Eddie a hug, and he squeezed her so tight she thought she would pop like a balloon.

In 1986, Cousin Eddie died of AIDS. "I felt the same way about his passing that he felt about Martin's," Gloria said. "I thought I'd never be the same. And I wasn't – I was better, much better, because of Eddie. He was an activist for black folks, gay folks, and forgotten folks."

Gloria now has three grown children of her own and has become an artist, launching a venture in which she paints "healing rocks" to sell and give away to children in hospitals, trauma victims, vets, family, and friends. She has found solace and serenity in the artful arrangement of splashing paint. "Sometimes when I'm painting," she said, "I imagine Eddie and Martin up there in Heaven together, laughing, cutting up, and singing with the Lord."

It is easy to imagine them, Eddie and Martin, looking down on Miss Gloria and smiling as she feeds her family that mouth-watering sweet potato pie on Thanksgiving Day. It is possible to imagine a world in which neither Eddie nor Martin would feel anger, fear, or resentment, just the love of their Creator in their hearts. As Gloria loves to say, the first ingredient of any dish (especially sweet potato pie) is love. And, of course, she learned that little black girl magic trick from none other than her beloved cousin, the fabulous QueenE.

Black Tights, White Tights

by Gloria Smith

(as told to Michael G. Hickey)

Her sister was eight, Gloria was six, and the year was 1964. They were unaccompanied minors traveling by Greyhound from grandmum's in Chattanooga back home to Nashville. Getting fidgety on a bench while waiting inside the bus terminal, Gloria was reading everything. She was a new reader, the best in first grade, and excited to learn so many words. The door to a fantastic new world had been smacked wide open. That was what made her so eager to play her new game: "Read Every Word I See." That way she didn't bug her sister with the constant: *What does that word mean? What does that sign say?*

The sisters hadn't seen mommy for two whole years. She was a concert pianist and toured with an orchestra, but she was taking a break for a while, like recess for big people. Gloria couldn't wait to get to mommy's house and empty out the baby blue egg-shaped suitcase sitting next to her. Her grandmum was sad as she packed it that morning. She said it was time for the girls to go live with mommy in Nashville. Mommy would be so happy that Gloria could read now. She was breezing through her McGuffey's Reader faster than anyone in her class. Everything around her was starting to make sense.

It was hot and Gloria wanted a drink of water. She wondered if her sister was thirsty but didn't want to be a bother. She looked around and found the water fountains all by herself because she could read now. It was wonderful. She saw a sign – and she could read it! There were actually two signs taped to the wall over two separate drinking fountains: "White Only" and "Black Only." Oh, this is easy, she thought. She could do this all by herself. Gloria didn't need her sister because she had already learned about colors in preschool. She knew her colors very well. This was Gloria and her sister's lucky day. They were both wearing the right colors to go to the water fountains. Gloria had on white tights, and her sister had on black tights. Gloria tapped her sister on the shoulder and asked if she wanted a drink.

"No."

So, Gloria scooted off the bench and walked toward the sign that read "Whites Only," but before she could taste the cool water, she felt someone snatch her away by the collar. Her mean sister was looking down at her as if Gloria had just said the worst curse word ever.

"What did you do that for?" She pointed to the sign. "Can't you *read*, dummy? We ain't supposed to drink from that one. We ain't white!" She walked away pulling Gloria hard by the hand to go sit back down next to the luggage. She didn't even let Gloria get a drink, just glanced over at the other fountain, the one with the "Black Only" sign, and told Gloria without speaking (using that black girl neck-roll of hers), "That's the only choice you got, so take it or leave it."

Take it or leave it. That was the kill shot.

For Gloria, fifty-four years later, the kill shot has stopped reverberating, but the sting is still there. A lifetime of take it or leave it, an entire childhood walking to school past an old ramshackle country store with a sign in the window: *No-Dogs-Negroes-Mexicans*. A black girl wearing white tights… Take it or leave it. A lifetime of Should I play the race card? Should I let the race card play me? Were those really her only choices? Take it or leave it? *Take it or leave it?*

The Miseducation of a Negro Girl

BY ASHTON CYNTHIA CLARKE

The eight-year-old Negro girl at the hallway water fountain holds her braids back to drink more comfortably. Her richly melanated skin contrasts crisply against the stark white blouse of her school attire.

It's the early 1960s—in a very integrated elementary school in a very integrated New York City neighborhood.

Two of her classmates approach and wait their turn. One girl, who is white, points at the girl at the fountain and proclaims (deliberately loud enough to be heard across the hall), "Isn't she so **black**? Not getting an immediate response, she stares at her friend, who is also Negro but has a lighter complexion than the girl at the fountain.

After a beat, the Negro friend chimes in, "Yes! She's so **black**." And the friends snicker and chant: "So black, so black, so black!" Until the first girl finally looks right at them and, saying nothing, walks away.

That evening, the mother of the taunted girl makes a telephone call. **My** mother answers our phone.

Mommy often shared this event with close family: "And Myra's mother actually called my house! Of course, Cynthia promised me she had done no such thing! Why would my child call another girl black?! Cynthia is black herself! Chuh!" Mommy punctuated her story with Jamaican slang.

But I had lied to Mommy. I did it. I called Myra black. But she was black, after all. So, what if her hair hung longer and straighter than mine? I had heard about something called a "brown paper bag test." And even though my skin wasn't as light as a paper bag, I wasn't as dark as Myra. We weren't the same!

Besides, I was with my best friend. I had to agree with her! And that made it all right.

By the time I entered seventh grade just four years later, I was no longer a Negro. I was capital B - Black. We all were. Whether dark brown, redbone, or green-eyed with one white parent, we were all calling ourselves Black. Then, during my first year in college, I visited Myra at her home. I was sporting a blown-out, picked-out Afro, living in the Black House on an otherwise predominantly white campus, and protesting a college production of "Show Boat" for its cultural racism. I hadn't seen Myra since grade school. She never brought up the water fountain incident and neither did I. I figured my education in Blackness made up for my shameful behavior way back.

I just prayed she couldn't make out the guilt lurking behind my aviator glasses.

Many in my generation still find it hard to explain the miseducation we went through as Black people in America. There were no black dolls back when I was playing with dolls. Nichelle Nichols was one of the first positive Black woman images I saw on television. And Lt. Uhura did her job with style in that micro-mini skirt with her strong thighs! She worked in a multi-cultural—heck—multi-planetoid environment! Watching her was probably how I began shaping my own worldview.

Now, it's not like I had never been touched by racism. Once, strolling near the beach in Southern California with my mom, some white boys on bicycles—and they were boys, kids—zoomed by and called us the N-word. And during a vacation in Kauai, I heard someone holler the N-word as I drove along in my Jeep.

But I saw those as isolated incidents and didn't let them shift my worldview. After all, I'd divorced a Black husband and later divorced a white husband. So, I was an equal opportunity!

Even in my storytelling, nine out of ten had nothing to do with race. For example, my first online show back in 2020 was a charity event—a 24-hour "Zoom-athon," and I'd prepared a humorous narrative about being stranded at midnight in Los Angeles. Me—a recently transplanted New Yorker without a driver's license.

I logged in when the show started at noon, earlier than my assigned slot, to check on my host and support whomever else was in the show. Ten comedians and storytellers were in the Zoom room, no actual guests yet.

We'd been online for about ten minutes when the Chat box popped up on the screen with the all-CAPS words: "ASHTON CYNTHIA CLARKE IS A NIGGER BITCH!" What?! Did anyone else see . . . For one ridiculous moment I thought, is this someone I know, pulling some insane prank? But there it came again, "ASHTON CYNTHIA CLARKE IS A NIGGER BITCH!"

This was no joke. We were being Zoom-bombed. Then, over, and over: "NIGGER . . ." The word scrolled and scrolled in the Chatbox, repeating, and repeating, it seemed 100 times! This rabid racist had a dedicated key on their laptop, and they were just leaning on it!

This was only twelve days after the video emerged online of Ahmaud Arbery's murder. Like the rest of the nation, I was already raw and reeling from that. **Who** would do this to me? My mind was flipping along with my stomach. They called me by name. Yes, I know my name was visible on the Zoom screen, but they targeted **me**. They never mentioned the one other Black storyteller on Zoom. Was this someone from real life who hated me?

Wait – there's a fuzzy image in the bottom corner of the gallery. Was it –? "Turn off the Chat!" the other storytellers yelled. Our host was paralyzed. "Turn off the Chat!" Finally, the host found the right controls and cut access to the Chatbox. The perp left the Zoom.

Sweating in embarrassment and apologizing profusely, my host nonetheless had to ask, "Do you want . . . can you still do your story?"

"I'm traumatized and devastated, but okay." I managed to get that out, chuckling slightly as if it were all joke. I couldn't let anyone know that internally, I was bleeding out. The audience began signing in and I performed my story, like a real professional. I even hung out for an extra half hour. Then I crawled into bed and dragged the covers over my head.

For the next few days, I alternated between conjuring nighttime intruders in my bedroom, to huddling in fear on my couch. Silently isolating, I couldn't bring myself to tell anyone about the Zoom-bombing.

Somehow, I felt ashamed and guilty.

Then just a week later, George Floyd was killed. Another crime against my people, my Black people.

By then, I was beyond sensitive. Like my skin was flipped inside out on my body. That Zoom attack made Floyd's death feel even more immediate. A gut-twisting intimacy that I might not have felt otherwise. It was the peak of Black Lives Matter. And Karen-ism. And white friends wanting to be allies. But I didn't want to hear nothin' from nobody about nothin.'

Slowly, over the following months, I revealed the horror to a few friends. To convince them—and myself—that I could learn something valuable from the experience, I lifted a line from Nina Simone: As a Black artist, part of my responsibility is to reflect the times in which we live.

And from now on, my work would do that more and more.

But let me share with you right now the **real** story behind the story: I know that wearing an Afro back in college or writing "woke" stories now won't make up for the sorrow I caused an eight-year-old named Myra. My **brain** understood how horribly I had wronged her—**had wronged us all**. But until that Zoom bomb struck me, my **spirit** had never felt the pain of such a personal, frontal attack. It's taken me until now to acknowledge that.

So, I say now to Myra, to Myra's mother, and to my Mommy: Forgive me, my sisters. I am so terribly sorry.

THESE BLACK BODIES ARE
BODACIOUS

In this here place, we flesh; flesh that weeps, laughs;
flesh that dances on bare feet in grass.
Love it. Love it hard.
Toni Morrison

beautiful: a prayer

don't rage against the silence the alien
the whole whiteness of
the wall and its baked brick and stain
as pinched as that constant tease
but instead, cup each palm and sit back
cocked preening your back like a stick
breaking its own badness in its own
prologue of pride growing
groaning here hear me queen
wind sand mountain poem the possible
place that carries
the magic says you are beautiful
black girl you are wanted
by some other who takes your
speech always for song
and loves the sound of you
tune yourself to this the way the hole
fills itself with sugar
and the gathering of your
telling of it the world
you are how your
recognition is all their recognitions of how
your saving is all the world's redemption
take attention to every piece
and balance it confidently
on the top of your afro pluck its
the soft sheen of skin to
to puff out and seek the fruit juicy
and waiting that crop of flowers that
burn that palate with sweetness that
good dirt the color of the back of your
hand singing in your teeth making
everything
clean and everything in front of you glows
thick gold plates under and over the skin
around the waist inside
your breast kernels like little
grasping hands such good things
this self-love such good things
we are so beautiful
we teach we pray we speak
we've learned finally beautiful us
black girls and we want more
more please

amen

NIKIA CHANEY

The Wrath of Conk

by Angela M. Franklin

We nicknamed our dad Bass Fiddle because of his deep baritone voice. That voice would rattle your bones if you were doing things, you had no business doing. Still, he had a soft side to him, which would go unnoticed at times. That softness netted him a new unwanted hairdo to prove to Mama, our bootleg hairdresser, that she should not put the new curl relaxer product on our hair. It was probably one of many self-less things Daddy did for us that didn't seem much like protection at the time.

Anyone familiar with the politics of Black hair knows the torture we have endured since the first slave ship landed on American shores. Back in the day, Bass Fiddle wore his hair conked (permed) in the early '60s. Daddy, like so many other Black men, aspired to sport a white-looking hairstyle took to using caustic, foul-smelling concoctions made of lye and other harsh ingredients to straighten his kinky hair. I was too young to understand what conked hair was or how one achieved this look. All I know is Daddy's thick hair was unnaturally straight.

He sported a pompadour--heavy on the crown of his head, parted and combed to one side. The back and sides were slicked back or as they used to say dyed, fried, and swooped to the side. Daddy's do made his six-foot frame seem even taller. I remember people telling him that he looked like a better version of Nat King Cole. I don't know whether he liked the comparison or not, but Daddy was regimented about keeping up his hair. Every day after work, he would comb and pat it into place and tie a do-rag around his head, to flatten the sides. He was even able to comb through the pompadour using a regular comb, which wasn't achievable with an afro. Afros had their own minds and consistently rebelled against conventional straight hair tools.

Bass Fiddle's hairstyle was rather odd for the water utility worker job he held with the City of Los Angeles. He dug trenches, laid plumbing pipes, and performed other manual labor tasks. Still, he had joined thousands of other Black men who were looking to achieve a look they figured more acceptable to the ruling class, by burning their scalps with a chemical mix of lye, ammonia, and other ingredients whose names I can neither spell nor pronounce. Daddy's coiffure was that of a man who didn't dirty his hands; he sported a pretty boy, a singer, or a pimp look. Without chemicals, Daddy's hair was soft to the touch and grew out like ink pen springs, typical of a Black man's hair growth patterns.

When cries of freedom and power to the people began to permeate our Black community, many men abandoned their conked hairstyles and embraced their hair's natural state and cultural identity. The Afro or natural as we called it was gloriously reclaimed, as were braided and beaded hairstyles. Some Black women didn't t embrace their own hair as quickly as their men. Black hair then and even now continues to be political. Hot comb straightening and curling with hot irons of our hair was routine. Trips to beauty or kitchen shops were the norm for many Black women and their daughters if they could afford it.

Personally, I had never seen the inside of a beauty shop. Mama pressed and curled our hair every other week, and by doing so saved money because she was good at it. Daddy was also a gifted unlicensed barber. He regularly cut my brothers' and cousins' hair. My Uncle SM, Daddy's brother, would drop off his sons and instruct Daddy to cut the "flies" off my cousin Ricky and Sandy's heads.

In 1967, when a newer, less caustic commercial straightening relaxer hit the market, Mama wanted to try it out on our hair. At 13 and 12, my sister Adrienne and I were ready for Mama to try it out. She and Mama fought regularly when the time came for hair maintenance. Still, getting the relaxer on our heads was rapidly being defeated and we were not happy with Bass Fiddle. He and Mama argued over the do-it-yourself relaxer kit because he said our hair was too fine for the harshness of the lye-based product.

"I don't want you putting that shit on my girls' hair," Daddy said. "Those chemicals are too strong and likely to burn their tender scalps!"

"Look Murphy, I'm sure there's nothing wrong with this product. It's new on the market and I'm sure it's been thoroughly tested or else they wouldn't be selling it in the stores," she said with one hand on the hip confidently and the other thumped a long ash from a lit cigarette. She took a drag from the Salem, exhaled, and continued, "Look at all the other products Johnson and Johnson makes," she added sounding like a spokesperson without pay. "Besides, I know what I'm doing. The instructions are on the box. I've been doing Angie and Binky's hair since they were born. It's not like I'll be putting the crap on their heads that you used to use. Putting a relaxer on the girls' hair will save me time. I need a break from pressing and curling their hair every other week and so does their hair. Plus, they'll be able to go swimming without having to worry about pressing and curling," she added.

"Well, I don't care what you say. Advertisers lie every day just to get folks' money with their faulty-assed questionable products. I'm not just gonna stand by and allow you to burn my girls' hair and scalps with lye. That's all there is to it. I've used it and I know what it's capable of doing. Remember, I used to conk my hair, so I know what I'm talking about."

"Huh! How well do I remember that look and the women after you like moths circling porch lights! I never understood why, but I guess it was a phase," Mama said adding, "I'm glad that's over," patting Daddy's hair.

"See now, Sally, there you go. What I'm trying to say is I feel so strongly about you not using that shit, so I'll allow you to put it on my hair for a test just to prove what the product's potential is. If nothing happens, then you can go right ahead and do theirs with my blessing," Daddy said.

"Alright then, fine!"

"Fine! You're gonna see what I'm telling you."

Little did Daddy know how quickly his prophecy would soon manifest. He brought a chair into the kitchen from the dining room and sat on it. In preparation for her bootleg kitchen salon services, Mama draped a towel around Daddy's broad shoulders. Daddy crossed his long khaki-covered legs and lit a Kool cigarette. Mama took a jar of Vaseline and smeared globs of it around his hairline and the nap of his neck. Next, she opened the jar of relaxer. At once, a rotten egg stench scorched the kitchen air. The smell alone should have served as an ominous warning that dire consequences were just around the corner.

Using a long-handled black brush that came with the box of chemicals, Mama began applying the relaxer on Daddy's hair with nimble-gloved fingers. His coiled hair began to straighten and relax to the scalp. Eureka! After about 10 minutes or so into the application, Daddy started complaining of his head burning. He ground out his cigarette in an avocado green ashtray and said, "Shit, I think you'd better rinse this out now. It's burning like hell. Ooo wee, it's burning like hell!

"According to the instructions, it's not time yet."

"I don't care what the instructions say. I can't take it anymore."

"All right, Murphy, okay. Hold your head over the sink, so I can rinse it out."

Daddy quickly obeyed her. We watched as she washed out the perm and saw some of Daddy's hair melting off and flowing into the kitchen drain trap with the white frothy relaxer. The mix of hair and foam-rich chemicals resembled a scoop of vanilla ice cream sporting a hairy topping.

After Mama's rinsing and washing, Daddy's head resembled a haircut executed by a blind five-year-old unleashed with clippers. There were bald patches and tufts of hair here and there. He took clippers and shaved off the remaining hair. Before that, a few strands left that managed to remain on his head were indeed straight, but the patchwork quilt look was quite damning. Baldheads at the time weren't too fashionable. I don't know where to lay the blame for what happened. One thing is for sure, it was either the product, the hairdresser, or both.

So, for six long weeks, Daddy sported the clean-shaven look under a baseball cap when he wasn't wearing his construction helmet to work. His valiant sacrifice was a six-week reminder of what most likely would have happened to our hair. The missing hair made Daddy's high cheekbones more pronounced and facial features larger. I never heard him tell Mama, I told you so, but his baldhead preached a silent six-week sermon we remembered a long time.

Looking back on that incident and the countless times we had to sit still while Mama's pressing comb started at the nape of our necks and continued above our ears until our head of hair was flattened. We had to sit absolutely still as she applied small fingertips of Dixie Peach or Royal Crown hair grease on the kinky parts of our hair. We'd hear the grease sizzle and pop, and watch it bubble through the pressing comb's teeth. The heat of its spine near your ear convinced you to sit still. And I tended to be fidgety.

I can't recall the number of times I had a slug-looking burn on the top of my ear or forehead. Recalling ear and forehead burns reminds me that the act of pressing hair is a somewhat dangerous and violent practice against our hair. And for what? To make ourselves more acceptable in someone else's eyes? If we don't straighten our hair, we buy it straightened and have it sewn or glued to our scalps. Well, if you can't grow it, glue it or sew it! I don't knock Black women for their straightened hair. That's their choice. The human hair industry is a multi-billion-dollar business, and the Black community contributes heavily to it. Under lock and key and armed guards, human hair is sold in various textures to customers willing to pay thousands for long, silky straight hair, that looks unnatural. But to each her own. I love being natural.

By the way, I don't think my sister or I ever thanked Bass Fiddle for his sacrifice.

Sometimes when we recall what he did, we throw back our heads and have a good hearty laugh just like he would have done.

SYKWMY

BY DUAN KELLUM

Jaffreys

BY AKUA LEZLI HOPE

Where she went to get her hair done
magic decades before the chemistry
became commercial and known by all,
sold even in small-town grocery stores.
There I learned the deep, wide secret:
that disparaged coil was not ours alone
Amidst the drone of beehive dryers
women of all colors and classes
reclined, lines of breasts, hills
and mountains beneath aprons,
heads cradled over
in long rows of sinks
or netted beneath cone hat
dryers, the roar and smell of negotiation
frowzy manes, clouds of coils,
coppices of kinks maimed
straightened, americanized, tamed.

my hair is natural dammit

(i can stand the rain)

BY JACQUESE ARMSTRONG

i come from a long line of strength
developed from genes that
travel back to a ship
where survivors were born
only steel-trapped minds survived on
morsels of hope
self-directed pride

the synaptic matter jails me though
reminds me of a cell
where fannie lou hamer suffered
blows to almost death and
the places where many
lost breath
through centuries' mass white psychosis
and delusional reigning kings/still do

so
when irrationality turned on me intimately
had to decide
the crossing bridge
knowing i live to tell
the punitive tales

i must tell the babies
how i got over
what i got over

this is my destiny
my righteous truth

the challenges' singular
perspective air
advantages pre-measured

those who claim privilege

yield distracted compounds and
time is the empty chair that sits
alone in the corner
it is irreverent and barren
like the trees in frigid winter
(you must breathe)

the rain beats down at
times shouts its
evolutionary silence in thunderous
roars
rebirthing curl patterns
introducing growth

but my hair is natural
i can stand the rain...

Powerless

by Stephanie Liggins

A white woman pulled my hair today,
and just like that she fell from grace.
She used to have a name,
used to be my instructor,
used to be someone I thought of as kind,
helpful, friendly even—
until she pulled my hair.

She didn't pull my hair like a yank
as a sign of aggression.
It was worse.

She grabbed it like
she was about to put it in a ponytail.
She grabbed it like
she was my mother, my sister, my cousin
who was about to scratch my dandruff.

Uninitiated, uninvited—forced intimacy!
If she had groped me,
it would have been kinder
because then everyone would understand

that I had been violated.

No one would question if I was too sensitive.
They would know

who was wrong, what was wrong, why it was wrong
and be aghast.

This way, I too, am condemned.
Too sensitive
in the eyes of the citizens of the world around us.
Because they look like her, think like her,
they can touch without asking
because they are who they are.

They don't touch each other's hair.
They don't pull each other's hair.
Why pull mine?

Because it is different.
Because they are curious.
Because once they examine it,
they can conquer
yet another new frontier.

As a Black woman with locked hair,
I am a novelty,
an enigma, a rare jewel
they need to subject somehow.

When she pulled my hair,
I was no longer a woman among women,
I was an object to be examined.

I was someone no longer in charge of
or in control of my own body.

When she pulled my hair,
she told me, I am superior to you.
I can do to you, and you can't stop me.
You cannot respond without retribution,
and the angry Black woman
stigma will be re-ignited like a flame.

If you don't like it,
you are powerless to protect yourself
now or later or ever.

Now, we can't be friends.

I don't want to be under her instruction.
I know her,
she does not value my humanity
as she does her own.
And I am powerless.
I am powerless.

One Day

by Camryn Stevens

"They said at this point, they aren't looking for any more models."

"No more models? Ain't that why they had a casting call, to look for more models? What type of shit is that?"

I nodded and looked at the ground.

"Oh Baby, I'm so sorry."

I felt a hot tear trickle down my cheek. I didn't tell her what else they said, specifically the part about not needing any more Black girls in their show. Mama had enough to deal with.

I looked up to face my reflection in the mirror of our apartment's only bathroom. I looked at my makeup, left over from the audition this morning, and remembered the excitement I had as Mama hyped up my look. She said I looked so good the Queen of Sheba would be jealous, and that the new lashes I had on were her new favorite.

The now runny mascara was painted down my cheek by the two streams of tears that had squeezed out. I picked up the roll of toilet paper and grabbed a square before returning it to the sink counter.

"Yeah, well," I replied as I began to wipe under my eyes. "I don't wanna hold you up."

"Okay," she said softly. She looked around the tiny bathroom before continuing. "I gotta get back to work. But I unthawed the tamales Ms. Terri made for us, they're in the fridge for dinner. If you use the microwave and make a mess, clean it up. Make sure you let CeCe out, she hasn't been let out since I left this morning, but don't let her roam too far down the street. I'm not tryna hear the neighbors complain again. And clean up this bathroom! It's been a mess since this morning."

I nodded at each task she gave me and when she finally stopped talking, I turned to face her. I was almost a whole foot taller than her, surpassing my tiny grandma by age ten.

She took a deep breath, grabbed my arms at the elbows, and squeezed. "You know, one day you gon be the best damn model the world's ever seen. Oooh you just don't know it yet," she said grinning and gazing deep into my eyes. She gave me a little shake before marching off down the hallway.

Standing in the bathroom doorway, I watched as she picked up her coat and purse and patted CeCe, our pitbull, goodbye. My grandma had been looking after me for so long, at this point she was basically my mother. A fiery old Black woman, Mama had full lips and hips, a slick, walk and an even slicker mouth. She was not to be played with; 5'1 but was raised in the backwoods of Texas with eight older brothers and three sisters. Her mostly gray salt-and-pepper colored hair was always pressed flat with a hot comb and slicked into a ponytail that fell down to her mid back. She was a force in a female body.

After she walked out the front door, I turned back to the mirror. Poking and prodding at my face, I looked for her in me. Her skin, weathered and wrinkled by laughter and long, sunny days of work and play, had the same red undertones as mine. It paired well with the rosy cheeks and pink lips I had worn for the audition, a look I had practiced all week after finding it in a YouTube makeup tutorial. Although our complexions were different, mine the color of coffee before the added sugars and creamers, hers like a peanut butter Girl Scout cookie, we had the same bones. The flat noses, high cheekbones, and spread-apart, almond-shaped eyes screamed 'Jackson', the last name we carried from her father's family. Anyone could tell a Jackson from a mile away.

I reached up to untie the ribbon which had held my hair in the high puff it had been in for my audition, relieving the headache I'd had all morning. I shook my head a few times, encouraging my curls to return to their natural state of rest. I looked at my brown curly afro as the sides brushed against my shoulders and the rest, unphased by gravity, shot up to the ceiling. Mama always likened it to those sun halos we saw at church on those manger paintings of Baby Jesus and Mary and Joseph. She never let me straighten my hair growing up, and getting older helped me understand why. Whenever I asked, she always told me that I wasn't about to lose my halo on her watch. I knew it was more than that, though. I knew it was so I would grow up loving the way I look, not trying to hide it.

I began to clean up the makeup palettes and stray brushes, the creams and powders I had left out in my rush and excitement this morning. I let out a chuckle imagining what Mama would have said to those casting people if she had been in my shoes. "What do you mean, you have enough Black girls for your show?" She'd start. "You mean y'all got a capacity on how many Black folks can be on your runway at once? All them white folks but y'all gotta put a cap on *us*?"

Once I finished and the room looked good enough to pass an inspection from Mama, I switched off the light and walked into the living room where I was greeted by CeCe.

"Okay girl, I know you've got to pee," I said to her as she ran circles around my ankles.

I walked over to the door, grabbed my key, and put the leash around Cece's collar. As I opened the door and stepped out of our second-story apartment, I paused before the stairs to breathe in the fresh air. Feeling the warmth of the sun on my skin and the slight breeze blowing through my curls, I knew Mama was right. One day, I would be a star.

Ngozi Nzuri

by XclusivelyTaylor

Identity Crisis

by Marcus Muscato

Has anyone told you that you look like Dr. Avery from Grey's Anatomy?

Has anyone told you that you look like The Rock?

Has anyone told you that you look like Derek Jeter?

Has anyone told you that you look like Jeremy Meeks?

Has anyone told you that you look like Harry Belafonte?

Has anyone told you that you look like Yul Brenner?

Has anyone told you that you look like Obama?

Are you Mexican?

Are you Hawaiian?

Are you Filipino?

Has anyone told you that you look like one of those Dominican ball players?

I've been told and asked all of these throughout my life.

I'm none of these ethnicities or people,
but who am I if I cannot even be seen as my own image,
and not just as a pleasant shade of brown?

my bajan doll still holds memories

BY DANA TENILLE WEEKES

i pause before saying the first name
of grandma, even recalling

her face, except our brown eyes. i have
not one photograph of grandma

but do remember her hands
in a Bridgetown store pulling

off a too-high shelf a doll
with blue eyes it never asked for.

blown out yarn platted into two like mine
when momma did it. like grandma's

skin i could never color right for cork
and tack art shows in first grade.

color smushed into an absence
between black and brown in my crayon

box. but there were blues and greens
for all those shelved dolls watching us.

"take her back to New York with you, eh"
grandma said. i named her "Molly"

after a girl i told daddy about every night.
a little girl in a different place who discovered

friends in a giant, yellow chatty bird and other
make-believes on a city street by the last page.

Born White

by KLARISSA CONNER

When the cute boy with ocean waves for eyes lands them
on my chocolate-colored pools,
He looks me up and down—for
the first time and tells me,
"You look different."

I do not cry…
Instead, I smile.
I ignore the strangely familiar ache in my chest,
      I was only 5.

      How was I to know what it meant?

Mom takes me to a salon.
Women with sleeked-back
hair straight and long
couldn't have been theirs fluttered in the room.
The place smelt of burnt sulfurous.

Next morning I'm in the mirror attempting to brush the frizz out.
I must have slept wrong. Was I supposed to wrap it? No one said?
I brush and brush, the 'do' now resembling a lion's nest.
Mom is flaring her arms, red in the face screaming,
"Oh, the money you cost me!"

I say nothing.
I stare down at my blonde blue-eyed doll and brush her long straight hair.
Fast Forward… I am nine,
A boy named Garet with spiky blonde hair embezzles my heart.
I gave him my recesses,

He gave me his packed snicker bars at lunch.
We laughed on the playground each day.
I did not mind the woodchips in my Skechers.

When spring rolled around, the changing leaves delivered Ashley.
Ashley was beautiful, I knew even at this age.
Her hair long and blonde. Smile so bright.
Her eyes blue, similar to the skies.
Her skin snow white.
Her face wore "accepted."

Garret began to spend his recess with her.
When I asked him why, he said,
"She's different, and I like her hair, and I like her smile, and I like her eyes."
Tone innocent and oblivious that each syllable split into my chest.

The words plunged into my heart,
I can still feel his mouth twist the knife.

I do not cry,
Instead, I laugh,
I tell him that he is a good friend.
I smile.

I go home that day,
Stare in the mirror and I cry.
I grab a pair of scissors and I cut my hair.
Patches began to fall at my feet.

When Mom finds me and asks why,
I ignore her questions.
I run to pick up the blond-haired doll and ask,
"Mom, why wasn't I born white?"

Am I not light enough?

by Klarissa Conner

Skin too dark for sun to blister
Don't want the fair-skinned
girls to feel inferior.
Bundle up.
Don't show too much!
Do you want to *look ghetto*?

Keep your hair in braids
just let them touch em,
play with them,
mangle their fingers through em
you're their pet-
I mean friend. Don't get mad.
Are you *that angry* black girl?

When they ridicule your hair's
coily texture, laugh with them.
Ignore the parts of you
that shrivel away.
Look, Think,   Maybe,
you're more *like them this way*.

Am I not dark enough?

Why do you push me away?
Terms become assurance
white-washed, light-skin
where I thought I'd fit in
my appearance remains

a burden. I am you.
I am still one of you.

What ethnicity are you?
I check the box, just like you.
Lighter shade or not
to the rest, I am stained.

Why you talk'n like that?
          Talking like what?

Why you dress'n like that?
          Dressing like what?
What you can't dance?
          I ain't got rhythm.

Am I not enough as I am?
The shrinking of my stride
and all that is me is worthless.
To all, it goes unnoticed.
I am either one or the other.
There are no parallels,
though I still exist.
I become what I have always
feared the in-between
I am what lies within whiteness and blackness
I cannot crumple myself to fit in either
I stand alone
in my skin.

KLARISSA CONNER

Soulstice Woman

BY DANIELLE HAYDEN

Do not run from rays.
Let them caress you
Let them soak your skin.

Be not exiled to the shore,
But headfirst
Dive into the waves.
Unearth texture's truth.

Head held high, don the most vivid of regalia
In bright hues, we've been told aren't meant for us,
So marks your coronation.

Never entertain a thought that you

Are not stunning in summer.

An Angel is Like a Patch of Grass

BY DANA TENILLE WEEKES

October 9, 2018, Washington D.C.

when you fall. The sun decided to rise again. Its orbit pulling me out of bed. Heavy. Like last night's rain flooding someone's basement and my slumber. I take a shower and cannot remember. I brush my teeth and have forgotten. I boil an egg. "Did I turn off the stove?" I remember my keys before the door closes and walk noticing a flattened plastic cup and a rat in a crosswalk. Weeds faithful in cracks. Smudged crap somebody didn't miss, though I'm sure they wanted to.

Beep! Beep! Beep! No need to look. I know the protocol of a catcall from its first purr. Beeeeeeeeeeeeeeeeeeeeeeeeeeeeeeeeeep! And sometimes you cannot ignore a roar. Only to discover an elderly Black woman stopped at a green light. "Excuse me," her voice says, cutting through commutes and resentment behind her. "Beautiful Black girl, walk with your head high." Then she races through yellow light.

THESE BLACK BODIES ARE
BEARING WITNESS

When we speak we are afraid our words will not be heard or welcomed.

But when we are silent, we are still afraid.

So it is better to speak.

- Audre Lorde

A Walk With Mom

by André Le Mont Wilson

In the summer of 2020, a four-mile segment of the San Francisco Bay Trail that ran along the San Pablo Bay a mile from my home in Hercules, California, provided the closest place to walk. It provided enough space for pedestrians to maintain social distancing during the COVID-19 pandemic. It also provided enough witnesses to prevent me from being stopped, chased, or shot for walking while Black in my community.

I strolled down Sycamore Avenue toward the waterfront. Protected wetlands bisected the neighborhood of apartments, townhomes, and homes. A dead eucalyptus tree stood on the edge of a pond covered with scum. Its grey trunk twisted skyward like a tree out of a Tim Burton film. Woodpecker and beetle holes dotted the tree that leaned to one side. A broken branch stuck out at a forty-five-degree angle. *That's a lynching tree*, I thought.

As recounted in her self-published autobiography, *Yeller Gal: Memoir of a Sharecropper's Daughter*, when my mother, Jessie Lee Dawson-Wilson, grew up in Somerville, Texas, before World War II, she and her sister sometimes stayed too long when they stopped at Cousin Ruby's to watch her sew or at Mrs. Wade's to play with little David. The sisters should have been bringing the cows home from the pasture.

One day, their Mama accompanied them. She walked her girls and their cows, Old Black Gal and Rosie, past the separate White and Mexican cemeteries. Reaching a bridge over a small creek, Mama stopped and pointed. "You girls see that broken branch over the bridge?"

"Yes'm."

"White folks hanged a colored man there a long time ago. You see the grooves in that branch?"

"Yes'm."

"Those were made by the man swinging from the rope after he died."

After Mama showed them the lynching tree, the girls hurried home with the cows from the pasture every day after school.

When I saw that dead eucalyptus in Hercules' wetlands, I imagined myself hanging from it. My pace quickened down Sycamore to reach the Bay Trail and return by nightfall.

#

I turned right at Willet Street. On one side sat recent replicas of Victorian and Craftsmen homes. On the other side sat an original Queen Ann cottage on blocks. The weathered gray house surrounded by a chain-link fence had a two-foot gap down the middle. I saw the sky through it. Birds flew in and out. The city had cut the house in two to move it in sections from its original location. The house was for sale, for one dollar, to anyone who would relocate, reassemble, and restore it.

Years earlier, my partner and I had explored the home at its old hill-top location, which was undergoing redevelopment. He stood in the doorless doorway of the abandoned house and motioned to me. "Come on. Let's look inside."

I held back, worried that some guard might think we were robbing the house of fixtures and copper wires, but shoot me, the Black guy. But since my partner was a White man, I felt safe exploring as a Black man. The interior was a wreck. A thick film of dust coated the remnants from the previous residents, the last being unhoused people who temporarily found a home. Exposed walls revealed windows and doors that carpenters had covered during a century of renovations and additions.

The best features of the cottage were its original crown molding and its location on a hill overlooking the steel waters of the Bay. My partner and I fantasized about restoring the home to its former glory as stereotypical gays.

But the bare floorboards in front of the dusty fireplace kept drawing my gaze. I stared so long at them that I imagined seeing a reddish-purple stain develop like a photograph in a darkroom. I looked away, reminding myself that I was not in my mother's sharecropper's shack in Somerville, Texas, but in the Queen Ann cottage in Hercules, California. The two houses were not connected. My mother never lived in this cottage. I never visited her childhood home before its demolition for a widened highway. The only connection between these two homes was a story she wrote in her memoir.

An unused fireplace stood on the west wall of the shack where she lived. Whenever she, a girl, got on her knees with a bucket of soapy water and scrubbed the wooden floor before the fireplace, a reddish-purple stain appeared. "Mama," she called, "why does the floor always turn red whenever I scrub?"

Mama came from the kitchen and replied, "A man had been shot there years ago. He bled to death, right on the spot you're scrubbing now." Acting like her family got a bargain, Mama added, "This house was empty for a long time before we moved in."

Too scared to ask more questions—"Who was the man?" "Who shot him?" "Why?"— the girl remained silent. *I'm living in a house of a dead man. Could what happened to him happen to me? What if the shooter is still out there?*

As the floor dried, the spot vanished like disappearing ink.

#

I grew uncomfortable in the living room of Queen Ann and hurried my partner from it. Part of me wanted to pour water in front of the fireplace to see if a bloodstain would appear, like the one at my mother's fireplace. But, like her, part of me didn't want to know whether a man had died there. I reminded myself that my mother's shack and this cottage were miles and years apart. The stories of trauma we tell each other and pass down from generation to generation are their own form of haunting. They materialize like ghosts, disappear, and reappear again. But the hauntings never cease.

My memories of exploring the abandoned house sharpened after three armed White men chased and murdered the Black man Ahmaud Arbery in Satilla Shores, Georgia, on February 23, 2020. While jogging, he had explored a house under construction, and they assumed he had burgled it. I'm not surprised that before Arbery's visit, a surveillance camera filmed several White people visiting the same house, but nothing happened to them. A lynch mob didn't chase and kill them. I knew that there were two Americas, that Whites could do things that Blacks would be punished for doing. My America is not considered American but foreign, the Other.

I can now articulate the anxieties I felt while visiting the Queen Ann. I'm also aware of how I exploited my privilege. My White partner gained me access and a level of security in exploring abandoned or partly constructed homes in Hercules. This privilege is a legacy of slavery in which my partner is cast as a White master and me as his enslaved Black servant. Had he been Black like me, I never would have set foot in the house with him.

Passing the Queen Ann on my way to the waterfront, I also named the unease I had felt in front of its fireplace. I had seen myself shot to death for trespassing, bleeding out onto the wooden floor in front of the hearth. I imagined what my mother must have wondered about the man who died in her home. I also recalled my musings about Ahmaud Arbery. *Could what happened to him happen to me? What if the shooter is still out there?*

I realized I was walking alone on this portion of my route to the waterfront. I constantly checked my surroundings for any signs of armed White men in pickup trucks. I speed-walked to the Bay Trail.

#

I arrived at the waterfront. New apartments with views of gray waters stood and awaited occupancy while other lots awaited construction. I walked north across a bridge to join a section of the Bay Trail.

I had assumed that only Whites used the trail, but the number of Blacks and other people of color I saw surprised me. Two Black women walked and chatted behind face masks and sunglasses. A Muslim mother in a hijab walked with her child. A squad of Latino boys rode bikes. A cycling Asian couple played Chinese opera from a smartphone affixed to the handlebars. A Sikh man strolled; his maroon sunglasses matched his turban. And then there was me, a Black gay man. These were the people most attacked in our country after the 2016 election and during the pandemic. Like me, did they come to the Bay Trail because they felt unsafe walking in their neighborhoods? I noticed the erectness of people's strides, like the Black Lives Matter marchers coursing through our cities during the summer of 2020.

As wide as the paved trail was, I sometimes stepped aside and walked in the dirt to allow people to pass while maintaining social distancing. When my mother grew up in the Jim Crow South, she would step off the sidewalk when White children approached. If she didn't get out of the way, the kids would bump her off the sidewalk. She began carrying a sharpened pencil. If the kids bumped her, she left some lead in them. If my mother were alive today, what would she think if she saw her son walking in the gutter in the Golden State, even for social distancing reasons?

#

After walking two miles while wearing a face mask, I found breathing hard. It felt like someone was holding their hand over my mouth and nose. I kept thinking, *I can't breathe. I can't breathe.* I wanted to rip off my mask and inhale the wind whipping off the Bay but feared people would recoil from me as if they had seen the Phantom of the Opera ripping off his mask.

But then I thought of the other man who said, "I can't breathe," as he lay dying under a policeman's knee in Minneapolis.

To this day, I have not watched all eight minutes and forty-six seconds of Darnella Frazier's video of officer Derek Chauvin asphyxiating George Floyd. I have my own memories, stories passed down for generations, of my ancestors suffering horrific violence at the hands of Whites.—During slavery, my great-great-grand-mother's owner and father threw an ax at her head to stop her from running away. The girl had incinerated in the oven the black house cat the Missus had named Nigger to spite the mulatto daughter of her husband. The girl survived her head wound. During Reconstruction, my great-great-great-grand-father was tied to a railroad boxcar by the Ku Klux Klan and set on fire. He had axed to death a White man who had been trespassing on his tobacco farm to molest his daughters working in the field. The grand-father died from his burn wounds.—While I was not present at any of these incidents, these stories form virtual "videos" that constantly replay in my mind in a loop. Seeing a barren tree, an empty boxcar or an abandoned house triggers these unbidden "videos." I can't turn them off.

On a Wednesday evening, just before Halloween 1988, Mom and I sat in the pews of First Church of Christ, Scientist, San Fernando. As often is the case, one person's testimony of answered prayer sometimes inspires another person's similar testimony. Sort of like a story swap. On that evening, after one woman stood and testified of praying to find a lost wedding ring, another woman testified of praying to find a ring lost in a dust storm.

Sitting beside Mom, I sensed rising energy radiating from her body like electricity. She too, wanted to stand to testify before the congrega-tion of a similar story about a lost ring. But biting her lower lip and clasping her hands, she remained seated and silent.

Either on the way home or just after we arrived, she told me the testimony she couldn't tell in church. "My Mama once told me a story about a lost ring."

"What happened?" I said, hoping for another inspiring testimony of faith.

"Well, there was this well-off White woman in Texas . . ."

"What part of Texas?" I asked, preparing to record her story in my diary the moment she finished.

"I don't know. It was somewhere southeast of Somerville. My Mama heard about it. So, one day, this rich White woman lost her diamond wedding ring. She looked and looked but couldn't find it. The only other person in her house at the time was her faithful Black servant. She confronted him and said, 'Where's my diamond wedding ring? You took it.' And he said, 'No, Ma'am, I never touched your ring. I wouldn't do such a thing. I've worked for you for years and always been faithful to you.' But she believed that all Blacks stole. So, she called her husband and ordered him to take her servant out to the country and hang him for stealing. Her husband rustled up some White neighbors and ranch hands. They tied up the faithful servant and led him away, crying and pleading innocent."

Mom paused for dramatic effect before proceeding, "So, this woman went about her chores, feeling that justice had been done. But without her servant, she had to throw out her own dirty water from her wash basin. And you know, when she did, she found her diamond wedding ring splashed out in the water on the ground. You see, her ring had slipped off her finger into the water when she washed her hands earlier that morning. Realizing her mistake, she sent a messenger after the men to stop the lynching. But by the time he arrived, it was too late to save her faithful servant hanging from a tree."

Mom finished her story with an upward-turned finger as if the servant hanged in the air beside her. She had a slight smile of relief because she finally got to tell a story she had kept inside for decades.

I was stunned to silence. This was unlike the inspiring testimonies of answered prayer we had heard earlier that evening. I can see why she struggled with whether to testify before church because her story had no upside. Sure, the woman found her ring, but it came at the cost of a Black man's life because of her prejudice.

The lost ring story stained me with knowledge about how America works. I could do everything right—be a mama's boy, a straight-A student, a model citizen, a valued employee, a "faithful servant"—but false racial assumptions and accusations could end my life anytime and anywhere. I thought about this in the summer of 2020 when news reports surfaced of an incident in Central Park. A viral video showed a White woman, Amy Cooper, calling 911 on a Black man, Christian Cooper, a birdwatcher who had asked her to leash her dog. She said into her phone, "There's a man, African American . . . He's recording me and threatening me and my dog." Had Cooper remained in the park when police arrived, they would have mistaken his binoculars for a gun and shot him. My mother's story is not just something that happened in the past. It's happening today under different guises. The lethality for Blacks is the same.

Although I live in California in the twenty-first century, I sometimes act as I live in the Jim Crow South in the twentieth century. I did not need COVID to practice social distancing from White women. I have my mother's stories, and the memory of Emmett Till lynched in Mississippi in 1955 after a White woman falsely accused him of flirting with her. As I walked up the Bay Trail, I kept my hands close to my body so I wouldn't accidentally brush a woman. I averted my gaze, never greeted unless greeted first, and tried to look small and unthreatening. I made subtle course corrections, recalibrations, accelerations, and decelerations based on the approaching pedestrians' age, gender, and race. But I gave the widest berth to White women.

#

I arrived at a section of the trail that widened to accommodate a viewing bench overlooking the Bay. On the asphalt, protesters had drawn in colored chalk a memorial to George Floyd in bold letters:

NO JUSTICE, NO PEACE

#BLACKLIVESMATTER

Had a piece of chalk been left on the ground, I might have added the names of my known ancestors who died from racial violence. Instead, choosing a medium more permanent than chalk, I wrote and published numerous poems, articles, and essays about my family's history.

Standing before the memorial, I thought about all the micro-decisions I had made to reach the Bay Trail. Be wary of walking in your neighborhood where Whites might believe you are a robber. If a White couple approaches you, pass on the man's side to avoid accidentally touching the woman. Never carry an umbrella because the police might think it's a gun and shoot. Usually, I'm unaware of these micro-decisions. But the murders of George Floyd, Ahmaud Arbery, and others have ripped the mask off my strategies for survival. I'm aware of them now and their toll on me. They're suffocating me. I couldn't breathe, but I kept my mask on and walked.

History of Survival

BY JAMES COATS

Double Golden Shovel After Patricia Smith

Asleep with eyes open, too afraid to dream. I do
be mindful though of all the ways to make believe or not.
Will my pride and joy last as long as I do? Will he be
boy long enough to see his manhood flourish. I'm still frightened
the future can't be paid with my blood. There is no permanence of
this moment, no word to contain all the feelings in the _____
To approach a space, walk backwards through the past as time is a threshold.
Witness that land we were promised appear, waiting is what we do.
Willing to give everything of value and what is returned is not
no gift, they give sinister blankets of infection, that how it be,
is what it is, chop down your tree, poison seeds to see them withered.

Jesus was sacrifices for our sins his father stood by
Moses however, was delivered from pharaoh by the
Him that holds all the power God in fact
named Yahweh in those scriptures. It's interesting that
mama found hope in the stories. I found pages of suffering in the
man's cathedral of bones, in the brutality of beatings offered to black's.
Black people must have been cursed, couldn't have been this man's
the Devil. I'm sorry I can't be what you want me to be mama
that quiet little boy grew up with a loud mouth spirit and I named
facts the face of my faith. Chosen to confront serpents, I'll battle him,
the lies, and the god he created. I wandered long enough even Moses
by decree never saw the promised land and Jesus
withered on that stake, like fruit hanging from a tree, how strange that is.

Be courageous I say for they will take and take 'til no more is left. No,
not even your breath is allowed safety in your chest. Those willing
do not forget the history of survival. I have seen it, witness
threshold between present and future the veil destroyed to
the detriment of those pitiful souls who will never find forgiveness. This
of course, is not the end that they had hoped for. Being one of the
frightened is no way to live and yet we do - live. My boy
be the best part of the rising sun, the jewel in midnight skies. He will
not be stolen or sacrificed to the unholy hands that have come to be.
Do I believe in protection? Yeah, my own, because God has been asleep.

Cornerstores

BY ERIC DEVAUGHNN

in 2018, Cornerstore Caroline accuses a 9-year-old boy of sexual assault. "Congress makes lynching a federal crime 65 years after Emmett Till"
– NBCNews.com

a boldfaced call put her in the world's stare
assume the brooklyn boy with snacks is all hands

    assume chicago boy's voice has its own hands
    somehow his words would claim the space of her

some howling words empty the space of us
on the boy's back, a bag full with learning

    "catch him in a bag, fill his back with learning"
    they plucked him from the softness of his sleep

she plucked from him his softness and his sleep
no child deserves to be dragged a name made mud

    no child deserves to be dragged and found in mud
    one mother woke to find these roles unchanged

another spoke, defined the role the of change
her call: Open-faced box. Put that on WorldStar

Breonna, I'm so sorry

by Davian Chester

What Would You Do The Morning After a Bombing?

May 13, 1985

BY DANA TENILLE WEEKES

I twisted the spigot
a few times and stretched

the front yard hose to a tight rope.
I needed water, a rush

even if from the interlopes of Philly's filth.
I needed something for the Solomon's Seal

leaves with pocks,
not from damn sawflies, but ripe ash

of drywall and black skin
huddled in a basement over on Osage Ave.

Just yesterday—a few streets over, girls
had been playing the final quarter

of their childhood. Maybe hopscotch.
Maybe skipping rope to *down in the valley*

where the green grass grows
Their skin becoming Solomon's.

Their ears, ours rope-slapped—metaling
helicopters. Primary colors whiplashing

against black belloooooooooooowwwwwwwwwwing.
Ashed girls, boys in backyards rushing

across rough bluegrass for mommas. City eyes calling
television screens, begging paned windows to a star-

less sky for saviors on Osage.
But there, those so-called saviors stood.

There never was a rush.
Not like water from a tightrope.

Learning to Run - Circa 2022

(4/23/22)

BY SHONDA BUCHANAN

"It" slipped into my morning tea and toast,
words like encroaching, artillery, forces mobilizing,

people fleeing. Flashes of faces streaked in tears and disbelief.
Even the smoking air was angry,

shuddering with each crash, each breaking,
each precious moment of their normal lives falling neatly apart.

But why were African and Asian students being thrown
off Ukraine trains when bombs were falling?

We are all learning to run again from the soldier with a gun
who doesn't care what we look like.

We are all hiding from a soldier, the boot-kicking army, the bullet,
gut-wrenching gas, the noose, the dictator, another master

seeking to end our dreaming. Who was on watch?
The world's collective question mark rising above our heads

could be seen from space. Because the "it"
has been happening in Africa, the Middle East, South America.

War kissing the faces of infants in their sleep
while we look desperately into the eyes of mad hatter leaders

who sleep with machetes under their beds,
who suck life from the earth in deep unapologetic breaths.

And the professors, the poets, the mothers and fathers cry
in our cars, in laundry rooms, in hallways,

watching the unfolding, smelling sulfur in the air
as we shop, eat dinner, tuck our children in at night,

make love, read poetry, begging them, let the innocent live,
let all our children flee. Stop raining shrapnel into our living rooms.

We are all refugees in war.
"Ukrainians only on these trains."

Reminds us that history haunts the present.
Marking me against the sound of missiles creasing the tulip sky,

kissed by a colonial past. I am again picked out of a lineup
because of the color of my skin.

Please. There is a war. These are terrible times. This is a terrible moment.
The flowers are burning everywhere.

We are all learning to run again.

Africa on my Mind

by Duan Kellum

en pleine air

by Judy Juanita

in 2019 merchants in
kansas traded memorabilia:
$324,500 for a quarter-plate daguerreotype
of enslaved people carting cotton
in woven wicker baskets

before we were memorabilia
skulls lips noses genitalia
en pleine air
we were perpetual mourners
grotesqueries
raw footage for the amerikkkan dream
displayed like godzillas
our scars filled daguerreotypes
as cannibals tore crisply blackened
skin from the sweet magnolia tree of life

ah! bourgeois shopkeepers photo'd in daylight
nooses tightened necks snapped posing
deathly polite *en pleine air* for postcards
like post-production still photography

the postal service wouldn't ban lynching cards until 1908
the business of slavery being business
brisk then brisk now
as daughters of the amerikkkan revolution erected
high monuments to remind *the nigras* of their proper place and posture.

for some odd

BY PAMELA PETÉ

footnote

emaciated   some more dead than alive   threadbare or without clothing   i did not witness it then   i
witness it now   time doesn't distance   the knowing   hearing   jumping overboard better than
bondage   the red and yellow screams   imbedded   dripping down the ship's hulls where bodies
dead and alive   mothers   fathers and children lay sandwiched between each other   on all
bodies fluid and waste   wasting away sailing away way embedded in the hulls   molding wet
dank dark that swelled inside them   before bursting into lost children   husbands   brothers

mothers   no name no pride   nothing to hold onto   exited slave ships   listed as 20 and some odd

Dear George

by Veronica Evans

You didn't know me, but had we been at the same places at the same time, we would have crossed paths. You are my father, my neighbor, my friend, my son.......and now, in death, much, much more.

Everywhere I look, even when I'm not really looking, there you are, struggling but hopeful.

Everyone claims to know you......now. Those who never knew you then, nor wanted to know you, didn't see you then, now claim to wish they had. And I imagine there were those who knew you but for shame, claimed back then that they didn't. No one admits to knowing someone who stumbles not just once, but many times, even though that one rises from the ashes to scratch out something new, hoping it will last and be the 'up and out' of the maze of false American life.

Some who are trying to grasp at every corner of your life are defining you, like little bites of sweet out of a whole lot of bitter: child of God, convict, complicated man, fighter, mentor, OG, parent, rapper, star athlete, strong and typical. Isn't that how we are all labeled? Christians say we start out as a child of God and end up typical without any acknowledgment of the spark of greatness lying close to the surface, just not close enough to explode up and out.

What happens in between is no one's concern or worry, especially those who, for their own ego or sanity, must find a box for you to fit in. Yet they vastly miss the prime point, you are in the biggest box of all, a Black man in this America from a heritage of Black wealth hard fought for and attained by your great-great-great grandpa, Abram Stewart, and your great-great grandpa, Hillery Stewart, both born into slavery.

Your strong sense of self, despite all the trials of Black life, came from both the white and Black Stewarts, as proven by the white slave owner Charles Stewart, who himself was an indentured servant and later passed along to his grandson, Joseph Stewart.

Yet, like most Black people, fighting hard and long didn't hold on to that wealth thanks to an unloving America full of rigged systems causing all our parents to humbly be 'just getting by'.

As I look at your image, now forever frozen in my mind, I wonder if you even knew of this ancestral pride and spirit, and from wince, it came.

So it is in death that you not only freed yourself but freed me as well. And I never want to forget the other face, the one to which was attached that other look, the gleeful almost playful look accompanied by the knee on your neck as you struggled to breathe free. And on the cold, rough concrete of Black life, your look of pain, and pleading for, what I believe you knew to be, your final moments of life.

Many did not want to bear witness to this, to confront what they deeply felt it to be, an insignificant moment in yet another seemingly worthless Black life. Yet as a mother, my heart and soul begged me to participate in honor of and for you.

I've known and loved many a Black man but only a few have remained in the center of my life. Through your own sheer will, never to be forgotten at any stage of your life, you changed so much about me.

My fear grew greater for my only son while I was trying to hold on to hope growing stronger for better times than my own youth had seen. My spirit of challenge and justice stood a little taller, and my writing, forced by a piercing need, took up different words and angles, determined to hold open the gate your cries pried away from my complacent life. I am so sorrowfully filled with guilt.

I thank you, Dear George, for taking your own unplanned place in American history, a history many of all hues will most likely try to forget because we created that and many other moments of terror and destruction.

I vow never to let your precious life be just another 'remember when' but a 'why we must remember', to which our answers must tangibly reply in every way possible based on the uniqueness of each American.

Rest in profound peace, Our Dear George
Our son of many mothers
Our uncles
Our friends
Our boyfriends
Our husbands
Our life
Our greatest joy
Our Black Man

Stilled-life: Ahumaud Arbery

BY JOANNE MCFARLAND

Not Tested on Animals

BY GINGER GALLOWAY

I listened intently
Suspended Blood clots
UNRESPONSIVE
The voice echoing in the recesses
Of my brain
A record on yellow card
Stamped dates
I won't take a second one
Reactions that feel like death
Looming
Dark eyes and rapid heartbeat
History shrouded in disease
Implanted in the blood of
Healthy men
Reduced to infecting children
The way they exercise warfare
Not tested on animals
Tested though.
Human monkeys
Mice
Guinea pigs
This headache
I get headaches
Unbearable
Avoiding light
Sound

Trying to crawl away from the pain
Between my eyes
Unable to read the medicine bottle
The house has become my refuge
The virus traipsing up the walk
Knocking
A syringe around my neck

i knew they would undo me

by Akua Lezli Hope

i knew they would undo me
this day before Thanksgiving
remove my layers, unbutton my sweater
i refuse to have my velvet coat
bundled against mucktreaded shoes

"this is so nasty," i protest
"we wash them every night and it's 5:30 a.m."
the uniformed woman informs
by way of comfort or agreement

i look down at the filthy public floor
i must walk across in socks,
the checker pats me down and pauses,
people look away as I raise and spread
my arms like a bird
the humming electric wand
is waved up and down my legs and then between them

It cannot read what gathers there
"Is it okay to lift and separate
each breast in public?"
No.   so grey trays of me
are carried to a small, shuttered room
and I am fingered in private
to keep America safe.

Is She or Isn't She: A Conversation

BY LYNDA V. E. CRAWFORD

Scene: Rushing to leave Catalina early. An East Coast friend, having realized not every island sways like the blue surrounds of the Caribbean Sea.

Me: We can wait for our later boat (pre-booked, General Boarding) or upgrade to First Class and leave now.

Friend: Let's upgrade and go. This isn't what I thought. It sure ain't Saint Kitts.

Scene: We stand abreast, chatting. First ones in the First-Class line; California heat in our nostrils, coconut water, and guinep ackee in our memory mouths. A woman interrupts.

Woman: This is the First-Class line.
Me: Yes, it is.

Woman: You know this is the line for First Class, right?
Me: Yes, of course. (my eyebrows say 'hmmnn I wonder, is she OK?')

Woman: Stares—in stunned righteousness.
Me: Stare—in peculiar perplexity.

Scene: My Friend pinches my arm. A habit she inherited from an Alabama ancestor.
One she's bestowed on me throughout our friendship.

Me: What?!??!! (triggered by the pinch)
Friend: Racist (breathed in a whisper)

Me: Good grief (exasperated whisper)
Friend: You never believe me; you'll learn.

Scene: I turn to the woman. West Coast White American
(my coast-biased thought strengthened by her peach-toned arms, yel-
low ponytail)

Friend: Still pinching; still ancestoring.

Me (to Woman): Oh, are you looking for General Boarding?
It's over there, you're in the wrong line.

Woman: (Silent) (That stunned righteousness I mentioned earlier).
She steps to the back of the now-several-people-deep First-Class line.

Me: (Silent) (Still in my peculiar perplexity); I think to myself Is she
a idiot—or wuh?
Listen closely and you'll hear my Bajan accent.

She's on Fire!

by Fallen Matthews

Post-Secondary EDI Myths and the Burnout of Marginalized Positionalities

I had my first seizure at night. I remember because, at the second of its onset, I found things akin to the dusk that unveil the fresh moon: wild crimson hues that birthed a crescent from the horizon. Nurses in the ER would tell me my skin was ashen. Aches would spear my temples. The pain would steal out of me in a matter of hours.

No one has ever figured out how or why that seizure happened. The same goes for the others which would follow. For over a decade, my MD had dismissed the symptoms I described; most of which involved memory lapses, joint pain, and mild, sometimes severe headaches. I was only recently diagnosed with a rare neurodegenerative disease (ND); a diagnosis I was only able to get because I had access to other doctors at my university's wellness clinic who granted me a referral to a specialist. While my seizures persist despite no anomalies on my EEGs, most have just likened them—albeit inexplicably—to my ND.

But I seldom think of my ND's pathology. What comes to mind is that it was only my pursuit for answers that led to its discovery. I can only attribute luck and fate as to why I am not currently mis- or un-diagnosed given my position. My pursuit never ceased to be anything but easy. The absence of ancestral records unnerved those in genetic counseling. If I could speak to my lineage, my neurologist wouldn't have had to order several other [painful] tests. But what little I could find from my elders and public archives had shown that my relatives were, like me, afflicted with inexplicable ailments and mortalities. That is the distant relatives on record. They were diagnosed with genetic disorders which drastically reduced their mobility, cognition, and lifespan. Yet, personnel today insist that their disorders are very 'distinct' and thereupon 'removed' from mine.

Not that I'm surprised the same complex that systemically disbelieves, and disregards marginalized peoples would ultimately overlook the roots of an Afro-L'nu woman whom it had also overlooked. Moreover, these roots are modest: bits I could piece together through oral history and public ledgers. These roots of whose harvest was pared, consumed, and destroyed by the same system that purports to cultivate.

This fucking imperial system: colonialism.

Colonialism is a blight that afflicts every people and land. The Manifest Destiny, genocides, and enslavement that underlaid the historical imperial complex disjoint me from my ancestors.

Moreover, its initiatives of Indigenous dispossession and assimilation must've endangered my ancestors as much as it demoralized them; inclining them to disassociate in real-time, in their own time. That disassociation ranged from lying about their Indigeneity to avoid being forced into what horrors would deluge them in residential schools, to their lives in sylvan isolation as a means of systemic disengagement, to disbelieving the merit of their positionality in which they perished with little if any totems to find.

The agents and legacy of colonialism plague me with imposter syndrome. They mark the skin I live in and what masks I must accordingly steal behind to survive; and they bastardize whatever or whomever they fail to destroy. Colonialism has befouled me as an imperial subject whose heritage is, was, and will remain denied in perpetuity by ideals of blood and cultural quantum; as if elements of identities can be minimized or bred out, because the whole cannot be greater than the sum of its parts. The dearth of kindreds undermines whatever claims I make to kinship.

I exist as someone and no one.

Those with claims and people may demarcate their lives and lineage. Even as they strive for reckoning, they are beneficiaries—and are indifferent to those unaccounted for—in their avowal of succession.

The identification and acknowledgment of my ND truly affirms that colonial models forever task those they displace. These models set quotas which they term to be 'standards of living' and 'respectability.' They are quotas precisely; they can only be cumulatively met and maintained through supremacist tactics.

This pursuit isn't my first and is far from my last. There are many ongoing and many which await. However, there are also many vacuous paths and people with empty objectives, to which I recognize that I mustn't (and cannot) strive to fulfill at the expense of depleting my own scant reservoirs.

So, I reflect on my current academic pursuits in which the humanities and social sciences are kind of a paradox. Theories and inscriptions are rather solitary although the interests of the masses underlie their objectives. This is a little different for me. Solitude and independence do reflect a lot of my own scholarship, but marginalization affirms how and why I make it a point to do many things in isolation. Positionality doesn't just inform me. It defines me. When it comes to the praxis and pretense of impartiality, it also nullifies idealistic attempts and assumptions. And, it drives home the reality that, despite how progressive, every community is ultimately rife with so many -isms and -phobias. This includes spaces that strive to empower marginalized peoples, particularly those who are operant on frames of the institution.

Which is why representation is a scam. The same disparities upon which the elites are contingent are the same ones that apply to skinfolk who assume authority within the institutional status quo. There are no "groundbreakers" or "trailblazers" who are operant within—rather than in resistance to—imperial regulatory systems. The avowal of those who 'represent' is why we struggle with the innate contradiction of traversing the violences of capitalism and marginalization; because, at the same time, we strive to humanize these 'representatives' whose empires are founded upon such. Your faves will always profit and laugh at your expense, but you let it slide because they're only 'human'; and [unpacking] that discourse underpins many efforts to establish the literal and figurative tolls of disparity. Some will argue the need to humanize everyone, including these 'representatives' whose come-ups come by through obliging—not gaming—the industrial complex. Likening them to be human, some say, is a part of the emancipative and reparative effort because dehumanization [and the belief that such evinces some existential or postmodernist superiority] is a testament to the evils which prevail.

To which I call bullshit.

These 'representatives' and their devotees insist upon the ethos of patriarchy, colonialism, and capitalism—in contrast to absconding marginalized peoples who repudiate those institutions. This betrays that these are convictions that they refuse to relinquish. They employ multiculturalist and futurist imaginaries because they are keener to merely *speculate* about utopian (albeit absurd) prospects rather than *actually work towards* them. This is why these folks can never reel in their adjacent. In the effort to humanize these types, people tend to overlook that they sparsely make space for their own because they strive to be distinct and therein arbitrate meaning at their own convenience.

In terms of academia, I find myself increasingly disinclined to pursue BIPOC and/or studies which concern marginalized peoples because of the aforementioned—precisely because most BIPOC and marginalized positionalities in these spaces are intended to enable and uplift colonialist praxes than those of reparation or change. Those of us who recognize and resist the principles of imperialism and capitalism firsthand—colonialism, patriarchy, and Amata-cis- heteronormativity—are precarious as is. It is nothing short of ridiculous to expect that we undertake the fruitless work of educating this system's beneficiaries. And it is *fruitless*: people are not amenable to conscience or reason when they reap the benefits from decadence or ignorance. When push comes to shove, they will not prune their privileges to weed out what malignancy comprises the root issues.

However, I understand the value of keeping humanity in perspective: it gives us hope; it reinforces the importance of life itself; it anchors us against waves of despondency.

But there are already insurmountable forces pushing me down. Rebecca will not be a monkey on my back. It also can't, won't, and shouldn't ever be on me to convince you to ascend from the Sunken Place.

As I write this, a particularly pallid and privileged person whom I have the displeasure of working with comes to mind; the progeny of a highly paid faculty and administrator who asserts that the systemic abuses and disparities we come by are through our own faults or choices.

Then, there's another one: the student who cosplays as the judiciary they aspire to become, whose arguments never cease to be facile since they are operant upon the assumption of an ideal world rather than the real one; as if the very laws they purport to uphold are impartial as opposed to being created, maintained, and even circumvented in the interests of hegemonic powers.

These people accordingly exemplify how marginalized peoples cannot and should not be held to impart their reality and urgency to demonstrably no avail. It's not that deep to them, the beneficiaries. But think of the depths in which we find ourselves sinking as we attempt to entreat or educate them. Our capacities (or lack thereof) to educate will always wane against these types of obtuseness since they are unwilling or unable to grasp the basics despite the abundance of teachable moments: and their commitment to inaction under the guise of tolerance and civility is just a means to manufacture apologia.

Bearing this in mind, I can understand why they keep coming back; why they can't disengage. They are unable to reconcile the incongruities which govern them; incongruities that render them unexceptional, so they're drawn to the lure of Others and they find themselves inclined to appropriate whatever they fail to consume or outright destroy. They seek us out for validation, sometimes invalidation; the former enlivens them whereas the latter vindicates their uncompromising monopolies. This is how they fool people into thinking they're "open-minded" or "progressive," except their trivial grievances are not remotely equivalent to our lived experiences.

And then, there's *us*: endless and eclectic, a profuse populace with something for everyone. But our vast niches also work to disjoint us. Imperial legacies foster this disconnect through remnants of ascribed castes and concepts of capital which frame our worth and self-concepts in terms of Eurocentric beauty ideals, disparate wealth, and productivity. We always fall short despite comprising a larger, more diverse percentile because we have yet to organize a collective, political dominion; and we instead acclimate to individualism only for anguish to make our needs manifest.

I often think of this as it relates to 'representation.' There are all these people who are well-known, widely read, or acclaimed; but despite the attention they command, they are bound to be overlooked and nonetheless impoverished. Understanding this is easy, but unpleasant because it articulates an unspoken truth: the absence of spurious or magnanimous imaginaries renders the bulk of 'ingenues' kind of unremarkable; as much, if not more unremarkable than we are.

Maybe that reflects the revelations which somewhat define how we grow up; revelations that hinge upon grasping the reality that everything is infinitesimal, ourselves included. And, maybe building up peoples and politics—upholding, living vicariously through their projected outputs— is both our accession and attempt to reconcile this fact. I often think of this in relation to activists and content creators in "marginalized" genres.

Another writer, whose anthology has received rave reviews comes to mind: featured in several prominent outlets and must-have lists, nominated for a few literary awards, read widely and locally—but still faces so much scarcity with so little support. I can't help but wonder if they are bound to become another statistic: paged off as paltry in the coming year but immortalized by the archivist who may one day stumble upon their work, long after its lure has waned. This person also reminds us how important it is to consider the significance of lateral violence since they have precluded the literary prospects of others, me included, and likewise, continue to disempower us as they instrumentalize their privileges and connections to a problematic vendor—in addition to just being a fucking Mean Girl.

Moreover, against the grain of this writer's alleged self-acceptance and luminescence, this speaks to the contrary: they have no real desire or power to change. This is why they commodify their positionality as a point of entrance and reference only to anguish as they sow discord. What is also telling is how I encounter mentors and elders who never seem to hold this individual (and others like them) accountable but manage to hold them in high regard—which goes to show that shared identities or struggles are insubstantial when it concerns uncritical reverence and social capital.

This marks the conundrum of being an outsider regardless of whether you're *inside* or *outside*. People would sooner burn everything to hell, including themselves, to oblige their faves or some prospective albeit improbable ally. People would also sooner light you on fire to keep themselves warm.

Whereas I am still reticent to admit who or what I genuinely am and likewise enjoy. I grow unnerved despite my survival as if time has softened my feats. I make a constant effort to be modest lest I be deemed too proud or burdensome regardless of what I am due. It makes me think of how similarly Others may recount their own trials and tribulations. More often than not, we are not afforded justice or closure. Despair seems to be all that is vindicated when reminiscence leads us to revisit our pasts, including our adversaries. Perhaps this is why we become increasingly curt and detached in our attachments or lack thereof: because we are conscious that this present is unlikely to be any exception, and that this present is likely to dissolve into the callous precedents of which we are familiar.

So, maybe that's how people get reeled into scams like 'representation.' Such concepts are reliant upon invoking nostalgia for a time, place, and being that never was. They build personae that are seemingly emblematic of who, where, and what we are in narratives. The key is discerning that these narratives posit these characters as 'valid' in a particular way: not as victors, but as objects worthy of consumption. In the industrial complex, it is the latter—*not* the former—which tends to cultivate guises of adulation and 'empowerment.' And the thing about 'representation' is that, unlike worker autonomy, personae are not taking charge of their intentions, nor do they revolutionize the parameters of dominant power systems. Once you grasp that, you realize that it matters not who wears the mask or enacts the pantomime since *personae* are not—and can never be likened to—the *real people* they purport to represent.

At their core, concepts like representation tether us to false positives, and how proverbs that caution us to consider life at large—such as "All kinfolk ain't skinfolk"—continue to resonate. Acknowledging this reaffirms my own strength and survivorship with respect to myself and my ancestry. So too does it incline me to remember from whom and whence I came; how the retention and assertion of this memory may honor its origins. That I may bear in mind which plots I have crossed and uncovered, what ground I have broken notwithstanding those who have led me to quicksand; and what morsels I have found and nurtured to fruition beyond and within.

1970

BY GINGER GALLOWAY

Polyester Houndstooth
Pants
With wide bottoms—
Bells
Ringing after class
Did you bring your lunch
Boxed
Milk, never white
Water, tea, soda pop, pee
Don't drink
from the last faucet.
At grandma's house
Snacks ain't sweet but
Sour
Pickles. Fingers in the jar
Your mama'll be here
Soon
Dinner will be in a silver
Tray in front of the evening
News
Of another Black man
Who
Is victim to the establishment?
Fists raised
High
In a revolution that doesn't

End.
Of homework from lessons we
Pretend
Are relevant to
Savages
Are what they called us in the
Books
Needing to be saved by white
evangelists.
Funny
The salve hurts so much more than the
Scrape
Your plate before you go out
Side
Of the house where the boys will take a
Turn
The jump rope one last
Time
To go in before the street lights
Catch
You in fleece pajamas
Gone to bed before the tv shuts
Off
Color jokes on late night
Racism
Cloaked comfort.

James T. 1952

by Karen Frederick

Thwop. A small trickle of blood ran down the side of James T.'s fore-head. Black shoes reinforced with steel in the toe, left over from his military service. Whack; right in the ribs. James T. rolled over in pain. He pulled himself over to the cold grey concrete wall and leaned back on it, his breath coming in spasmodic gulps. The blood that was coming into the back of his mouth made him gag. He looked up trying to focus on the nameplate, Stew something. The cop removed his hat, tie, and shirt and placed them neatly on the back of a coat rack.

"Git up; git up boy." He said.

James T. got to his knees and wobbled. He could hear the buzzing of dying flies on the windowsill. He grabbed the arms of a wooden chair and pulled himself up, bracing himself for the next blow. The door opened a crack.

His head hurt so bad he could barely open his eyes. The cop grabbed him by the back of his shirt with one hand and flung him around into the chair. James T. was almost ten but was so thin for his age he barely weighed ninety pounds. The cop bent down and looked into his eyes. He put both arms on the sides of the chair encasing James T. in a noxious fog of stale cigarettes and garlic.

"Hardheaded. We'll see 'bout that. All you niggers run together."

Whop. He hit James T. hard in the back between the shoulder blades.

"We'll see how you like it in lock-up. Bet you'll have a lot to say then." Captain Stewart handcuffed James's right hand to the chair he sat on. Then he walked to the coat rack and put on his shirt, tie, and hat. There was a knock on the door.

"Captain, his folks are here." The patrolman said.

Captain Bill Stewart looked at James T., reached over, and unlocked the handcuffs. He spoke softly in his ear.

"You got a free pass today. You won't be so lucky the next time."

James T. could feel his pulse quicken as the fetid breath of Captain Stewart washed over him.

"Yes sir," was all he could say. He wiggled his fingers to try to get some blood back into his hands and arms. The black patrolman who came to the door handed James T. a wet towel.

"Here clean up son; your mama and grandma have come for you."

James T. took the damp towel and walked gingerly to the small mirror over the wash basin and carefully wiped away traces of blood on his face. He looked over at the patrolman and smiled to himself. The policeman saw him smile.

"What's funny? You almost got yourself snuffed out and you laughing?" He said.

"Well, officer; I git my brains beat out when I'm guilty and I git my brains beat out when I ain't done nothing. Ain't that a funny situation?" James T. asked.

"Boy, you better keep them kinds of thoughts out of your head and out of your mouth." Patrolman Harris ushered James T. into the waiting room where his mother and grandmother were waiting.

"Mrs. Thomas, my name is Elwood Harris. This is the third time this month we picked up James."

Mrs. Thomas took a cigarette out of her cigarette case and lit it with a chipped gold lighter. She blew a puff of cigarette smoke at the ceiling.

Officer Harris handed Mrs. Thomas a piece of paper.

"This is my number on this piece of paper.

"We got a boy's club on 8th an' H street. James could come down and learn how to read and write better and maybe get involved with our boxing club."

"What I'ma call you with, we ain't got no telephone." Mrs. Thomas replied.

"Send James down on Saturday morning and we'll git him started.

He can ask for LD or for Mr. Walter."

"I thought you said yo' name was Eldwood."

"It is ma'am, but everybody calls me LD." LD didn't know why but he was getting a little warm in his clothes all of a sudden.

"The boy's club is for boys just like James."

"You mean hardheads?" She asked.

"Yes ma'am, hardheads." Officer Harris replied.

"We'll see." Mrs. Thomas.

James T. walked right past his mother without speaking and went to his grandmother. He helped her with her two canes. When she stood up; her back was so bent she could only straighten partway. She walked with a kind of rocking motion from side to side toward the front door.

"JT, you gotta cut this shit out."

"Yes ma'am." He held his grandmother's arm as they walked down the street to wait for the cross-town bus. Mrs. Thomas re-applied her lipstick and adjusted her girdle.

"Office LD?" She called.

"Yes ma'am."

"Will you be there too; at the club on Saturday?"

"Yes ma'am."

"See you on Saturday." Each step of her high heels on the hard concrete floor made a sharp sound like a pistol shot as she walked out the door.

a prayer to Godzilla

BY JUDY JUANITA

godzilla of the urban nightmare
godzilla of outsized space
give us this dream our daily dream
give us the dream of being
(the dream of supervision atop the dream of being)
nowIlaymedowntosleepIpraythelordmysoultokeep
We're trying to pray
oh my god/god my oh
god awful thoughts stagger (through) us
      gawd is a big fat showoff
      gawd is always late for work
      can we fire gawd for absenteeism?
oh my gawd is that blasphemy?

it's spelled differently
oh my god no no no no
andifidiebeforeiwakeipraythelordmysoultotake
gawdzilla doesn't have ears
is that on purpose?

gawdzilla likes catastrophe
cruel jokes
destruction
death and all the angels of death

cities on fire

scaring people to death
being a laughable hero
being mistaken for a hero
is that on purpose?

being a hero
calling himself hero of the world
going around the world
beating his chest
toppling buildings and governments
being benevolent after the fact

my gawd, he is full of himself
is that on purpose?

The System Isn't Broken

by Davian Chester

One Vote Will Waver

by Katerina Canyon

I have a ballot
Where choices are tied
To every side
But mine.
My candidates say
Captivating, hopeful things
But cannot work
Their way to redemption,
And I am withered
Past caring.

There Goes the Neighborhood

BY DR. MICHAEL ANDREW OWENS

Cruising to the stoplight,
I glance at a collage of red, white, and blue
Flags fluttering in a gentle breeze,
Waving for attention,
Banners tattooed with his name.

A pop-up canopy blocks the sun
From beaming down
On an array of paraphernalia,
T-shirts, caps, pens, paper propaganda
Bearing his infamous brand,
His noisome motto
Promising to

Make America Great Again.

The American Dream.
I thought I had moved far from the hood
To a quiet home
In a decent community
Where I could shop, dine
And safely walk for exercise.

What are *they* doing *here*?

Those people
Can make a corner anywhere.

Setting up their sordid commerce
For a commercial
To solicit patrons
Purporting to be infused with patriotic pride.

Who would have thought
Free speech
Would disturb our suburban tranquility?

As the Sun sets on another workday
Traffic picks up,
Instead of passing by to go home,
Curious onlookers randomly park;
Line up like they're at a ticket booth
For entry to one of those raucous rallies.
Why couldn't they wait for Halloween?

I might be inclined to convince myself
They're wearing his costume
With gold crowned mask,
Feigning interest,
Pretending to be that ignorant.

What are *they* doing here?

On an otherwise picturesque day,
I have to drive past their little shop of horrors
Or reroute myself
To avoid the skull and crossbones reminders
No place is paradise.

I navigate away from the alien landing,
Taking a detour into my enclave,
Thinking any day now
they will remove all signs of their invasion.

A stop sign orders a pause.

Piercing the view through my windshield
Into an amber sky,
Were poles protruding from the archways
Of 2 homes side by side

Twin banners hang
Advertising the same moniker
As the unfurled flags
At that other corner
Seized for his ominous enterprise.

Neither home had a For Sale Sign.

Junior Baby Meditates on Blame

(Hand Me My Griot Clothes)

BY PETER J. HARRIS

First off …

that's why we say *your* president
he might as well told them flag-smashing runaways from the human
    family

we love you Little Aryan

my poster children
my trolls
my ATMs

really he thinking: let a mob stalk a cop   break a cop   stomp a cop
long as I own the rights to pardon the storyteller

hand me my griot clothes

if people scared of this lifetime recipient of affirmative action

all I got to do is *squint* and become a cult leader in training
make individuals at a Lost Cause family picnic cower like they got
    Tourette Syndrome
make the Statue of Liberty herself tremble like a knock-kneed
    ingénue

truth be told some people so guilty
a one-year stay in every jail in the United States of America

for the next 100 years wouldn't be enough punishment

Say What ...

that's why I say first handle *your* business
start no further than your own day by day
mine & refine your righteous indignation

own up to somebody you let down   some unforgiving touch   some
    strangled praise
some grief we didn't feel

Black Life is ...
our planet   X & Y chromosomes   gravity of clean air & water
cry of healthy babies   freedom of reading & writing
pleasure of breathing & laughter   language of sex & love
more even than a gift from God
Black Life is
period.

You Know It ...

   clear your throat   quiet your babbling
   swim out of your silence

   who can say I have solemnly upheld my country's constitution
   without scrambling to avoid the lightning bolt from heaven?

   who can look into a newborn's eyes and send the telepathic message:
   I have used all power at my disposal to help create paradise on earth?

   who aint afraid to drop the top on the bulletproof limousine
   drive back roads of the villages supposedly part of your country?

hmmm hmmm ... hand me my griot clothes

whose underground bunker armed stocked and ready?
whose satellite set to unleash flying land minds and nuclear wel-
  come baskets?

who ready with new eyes now we given another opportunity to be-
  come promise?

we can all legitimately cuss out this or that people for crimes against us
speaking different languages   *... erryday, all day, any day ...*

(cannot take that lightly neither. we done killed each other. we done
enslaved each other. we done stole and cheated and spit on each oth-
er's graves and sacrifices and sanctuaries. *hmmm hmmm ...* all in the
name of love and god and *sacred he say / she say*)

well, sir, still the *beautiful* action that make or break a moment
honor the worst in our past we *can* make new history
change the way we imagine what it mean to be free
we *can* get more fabulous

listen: it aint just no one *nobody* and *no thing* done kept us from you
  better bet it!

we best to apologize about slavery and get to there but for the gift
  of grace go I
we best to find our humanity instead of making one more speech today
we best sip from the deep pool of *do right*
we best go ahead and *do right*

A Reflection on Spike Lee's Seminal Film, *Do the Right Thing*, or What Are We Really Doing for the Culture

by Denise Ervin

When Mother Sister stood
Barefoot in the middle of her
Burning Brooklyn neighborhood
And screamed at the top of her lungs
Only white folks thought
It was about Radio Raheem

Da Mayor's arms wrapping around her
Was Spike Lee's way of hugging us all
As though he'd know
All these years later
That we would still be begging
Our oppressors to
Do the Right Thing
That our collective breath would be stymied
By the knee to the neck of George Floyd
That we would add his name to
A storied list of lynching victims
That stretches as far back
As the distance of the Middle Passage
And that every lifeless black body
Would make it harder and harder

To pretend that our jobs, our degrees, our progress matters
In a world where black lives don't
Where we are everything but valued
Thugs, criminals, violent, felons, niggas
Where we take our lives into our own hands
Walking out of our own houses
Even sleeping in our own beds
I tell you
They will indict you for your own murder
While still drawing the chalk outline
Around your body
As if explaining why you deserved to die
Is part of the death notification process

We are playing catch-up in a system
That gave our oppressors
A 400-year head start
And a performance-enhancing drug
Called white supremacy
No wonder we're tired
No wonder being called strong
Feels like an insult
When you're a black woman
There is no shame in admitting
I have never possessed what it takes
To endure all of this
I am exhausted with being strong
With being loyal
With being faithful

DENISE ERVIN

I'd much rather be what my children
Are protesting for:
Free

I am Mother Sister
Wailing hoarsely at the racism
That predated me
And enslaved my ancestors
That gentrifies my neighborhood
And underemploys my children
Even when we give them names
That don't offend white sensibilities
I have said goodbye to too many of you
Have shed tears over black bodies
Both near and far
Both stranger and dear
And Radio Raheem was only one of them
Just as there is only one of me
But I pray there is a little of Da Mayor
In each of you
Because we may not have started the fire
But that won't stop us from getting burned

all of this

by Cory Cofer

We could all use a clinic on racism that's systemic
Which makes it extra hard to get ahead
You want blacks to sing the same tune as Dr. King
But in the end, y'all still shot him dead

Routine stops, routinely by cops
Result in routine, random stop 'n' frisk
Hands in the air! I throw my hands in the air
You get aggressive, though I pose no risk

Black bodies lay lifeless — they value our lives less
Irvin Landrum, Tyisha Miller, Michael Brown
Imagine the deaths when there was no witness left
And the only camera on was facing down

Black-on-black crime we're reminded of all the time
As if our problems are ONLY self-inflicted
When blacks kill blacks they go to prison
Cops rarely ever get convicted

If teaching standards evolve, medical puzzles get solved
then why can't law enforcement reform
When we take off these masks, I want a black middle class
We do more than play sports and perform

Hell

by Katerina Canyon

Justice, the scales are rising.
Inequality mars my resilient skin like bruises.
One million brown bodies of resistant winter join me
In the boiling kettle and drown.
Challenge this domination all together.
Invigorate my flesh.
I am not awake, but restrained.
When the closing bell of indifference rings,
I shall intend to remain in the smoke.
We are created equal,
But Justice
The scales are rising
And I can barely graze them
With my fingertips

stockton got black churches

by Cory Cofer

Emmanuel Baptist two-story
the drummer sang and played the piano soprano
too much ammo
in the hoods
before guns, black men fought good prayed good
blue-collar gigs paid good
life stayed good
before the gigs closed
unemployed on the corner spittin' flows
about being on the corner spittin' flows

Revelations: A Beginning

BY XAVIA-MARGRITH MILES

in those days we walked with god

half a step between glitz and fear

sermons in the magnolias

absinthe green plastics lit our way

to a world we dreamed,

lucrative opportunities, untapped markets,

every whim satisfied,

an organic-locally-sourced-cruelty-free
inclusive-campaign,

where the body be bread

and when it is husk—

fuel, for the god we trust.

Reparations

BY CHRIS "THE POETIC GENIUS" GREEN

Bound to an enterprise beyond our reach
America the kingdom, we're blacked out of a piece
Kept all the wealth and promised us peace
But put blocks at our feet

This is why they owe us...

This cotton got me dressed in the fabric of their lives
Still hear my grandfather's grandfather's cries
Stories of how they would divide
And conquer
Broke my family's backs and wealth
And well...
We still feel the hunger
Built this country from the south up
And west out
They count their blessings while we're left out
Enslaved us, freed us, and slave us new
Gave our father's prison blues
Give us dead sons, give our mothers heartache to this day
Fear wondering why the systems set up this way
Still overworked and underpaid
$120 billion dollar trade
Gave us Alcoholism to wash away the pain
Red wine on T-shirt, memories of the stains
Lost ancestors don't know where the remains
Birthplace of the crime scene I still remain

Kept our promised land and told me this the promised land
Still empty hands
But we demand
Reparations

This is how they pay us

Systematic equality across the board
Our skin the price for racism no more
Protect our women against death giving birth
Find out the loss to each family's worth
They know the percentage
Check our lineage
And send out checks
For every neck
They put in nooses
For every provider they erased from the family base
Look at the wealth made from cotton as the base
And pay
Freedom ain't never been free for us
Egregious
They act like they don't see us
We were cargo they never paid for
This country we slaved for
And they just made more
Give our families cushions to save more
Their generational wealth still in the hands of masters
If they benefited from our lives as stock
Tax them
And everyone that backs them

Everything silver ain't platinum
And our gold gon' glitter
Can't put a price on our soul
But our bodies were sold
And they should pay for that
Never should have gotten the treatment sheep get
Never again be seen as three-fifths
Government needs to be the accountant and the accountable
Or reconciliation is truly insurmountable
Sent out stimulus checks for the pandemic
Send out checks for our financial sickness
The once-captured, living fractures
Given fractions
Of our worth
157 years too long to be patient
Support HR 40 and band together our representation
Long live our freedom and give us our reparations
(Pay up)

Black Power

by XclusivelyTaylor

Monuments

by Chris "The Poetic Genius" Green

Bronze bodies get hammered into stone monuments
Whenever they gain momentum or glory becomes monumental
Ground into Hard Rock whenever we become instrumental
Until our history becomes pebbles in the rubble
Only left sentiments when we become sediment
Mining through our mental until our fault lines are their evidence
We asked to be grounded*
I struggled through the quicksand of fear to remain quiet
But my soul screamed riot
My burial grounds collapsed, refused to be another tomb with false depictions
Truth is, we live our narrative, we control our inscriptions

*

Dreaming A Reckoning

by Lynda V. E. Crawford

That ugly thought—
/we are a caste perpetual, beneath their feet /
could have been vomited
into your ear my love—or
tamped into our family circle-stress
deep enough to coalesce inside us.
Instead, we rejected inculcation
propelled truths into the air, crowded
with thousands marching, pressed up to polymer
power of the state, helmets – firm in our persistence
to cast out systems that keep us in self-doubt
& rob & rob & keep on robbing us of ourselves.
We've stopped fearing government guns
& covered noses unwilling to inhale our prescient smells
but destined.

Jim Crow in Koreatown

BY S. PEARL SHARP

Some forty years ago I unpacked my stuff in a neighborhood a lit-
tle south of Los Angeles City College sometimes referred to as East
Hollywood. My neighbors then were primarily Cuban, Mexican, a
growing population from El Salvador, and a sprinkling of white Eu-
ropeans. I seemed to be the only identifiable Black resident for several
blocks in any direction. Over the ensuing decades, I have lived near
Koreatown, then next to Koreatown, then in the middle of Koreatown
—without moving. Now I live in Little Bangladesh in the middle of
mid-Koreatown.

Walking a few blocks from my home in one direction I have a choice
of several Korean bar-b-que sites and a Bangladesh cafeteria, while in
the opposite direction, there is a Mexican bodega and sidewalks filled
with Salvadoran women in ruffled aprons cooking pupusas on little
temporary kitchens they set up each morning and evening.

By the mid-1990s Koreatown was in full flush and many of the
shops in my neighborhood began posting their signage only in Korean.
Some folks thought that was bad business, even discriminatory. Others
considered it an entitlement as Los Angeles now was home to one of
the largest populations of Korean residents in the U.S. The argument
became public, and some city councils passed ordinances requiring
Korean-English signage. (The same thing happened to the expand-
ing Chinese communities here in the 1980s, and again in Menlo Park
around 2013.) My take on the situation was that a Korean language-
only sign meant that the owners didn't want me in their store, which
meant I didn't need to give them my money.

But I do love to explore, sometimes wandering in and out of a line
of shops just to see what I might discover. From this casual curios-
ity I learned for the first time about the Armenian Genocide, fell in
love with the colors in Guatemalan embroidery and unintentionally
offended a sales clerk at a Korean pharmacy when I asked for a stan-
dard Chinese remedy. In a small Filipino supermarket, I was stunned

to discover a painful connection to my own community: skin bleaching. This social/psychological residual of colonialism allows that if your skin looks more white you might assimilate more easily into white society and reap its privileged benefits.

When a new Korean restaurant opened I saw that none of its signage was in English. Was it another of the popular Korean bar-b-ques, a sushi bar, or a tofu house? Unlike many of the other eateries that had dark signage, this one looked bright and inviting. Perhaps I could have lunch here or pick up a dessert. I was still experimenting with Korean food, but when I wander into food sites I usually try to order something. If nothing on the menu appeals to me I just ask for a container of rice to go. You can't go wrong with rice.

Standing at the counter it didn't take long for me to figure out that the menu was entirely in Korean. A woman who appeared to be a waitress or hostess watched me but said nothing. Across the counter three young women chattered rapidly as they loaded customers' plates. After a few moments, I asked, "Excuse me, but do you have a menu in English?" The woman sauntered away. The girls looked over their shoulders at me and began laughing, more like snickering. They pointed at me like I was a bad TV show they were watching, then went back to their tasks as if the TV had just been turned off.

Suddenly I was transported to a place I had never actually been, to a segregated lunch counter in North Carolina. In the 1940s, 50s, and 60s, at the height of Jim Crow segregation, restaurants had "Whites only" signs and even the outhouses were labeled "Coloreds." What we were shown on the news in the 60s were the most outrageous, most violent acts against Blacks who were demanding an end to whites-only lunch counters. But for each of those intense and sometimes deadly events there were a thousand moments like the one I was experiencing. No violence. No hollering. No name-calling. Just a spritz of humiliation.

My mind raced through a list of response options, but I was frozen in place. Why couldn't I respond? There were no Jim Crow signs in Ohio where I grew up. But from there to New York to Los Angeles I've been followed around by security in department stores, encouraged not to try on the clothes in dress shops, and told outright by white salesclerks in upscale stores that I could not afford the item I was looking at. I have sensed places where I was unwelcome. But this was different. They did not ask me to leave, they didn't say, in Korean or English, "We don't serve Blacks here." They just decided to not see me. Their actions said You Do Not Exist.

The thing about humiliation is that you want it to end. I gave the girls a hard, intentional look and walked out. But as soon as I stepped outside, I felt like I should go back in and challenge them, making it clear that I knew what they had just done. Or say --. Say what? I took a few more steps toward my car. Go back? Don't go back? Then I recalled meeting a young journalist who worked at The Korean Times newspaper. I had his card. I would call him, tell my story. Many racial confrontations are singular, dealing with one person's prejudice. But this was a group consensus, the blossom from a seed planted before those three young girls were even born. I would ask the reporter to put some light on an attitude that needed repair.

I found his card, but I never called him. I never called because, like so many other Black souls, I have wearied of teaching those of other races how not to be racists.

Now when passing that restaurant I still sometimes feel a flush of memory. There are race landmarks spread like measles across America. Some are huge, like the Lincoln Memorial in Washington, DC where, in 1939, esteemed contralto Marian Anderson performed a concert on the steps of the Memorial after being denied access to sing in Constitution Hall because of her race. And the Edmund Pettis Bridge in Selma, Alabama, now a National Historic Landmark where, in 1965, marchers pushing for voting rights were brutally beaten by state police and local citizens. Some seeds of racism are planted way west of the infamous Mason-Dixon line. Some markers are in shift, like the many statues of Confederate heroes and slave owners that today are being removed, or at least having their validity challenged.

But most race bias landmarks are unchallenged, unmarked moments branded onto someone's memory from acts devised by ordinary people in ordinary spaces, like a bar-b-que restaurant in Los Angeles' Koreatown.

THESE BLACK BODIES ARE
ECLECTIC

I speak to the Black experience,
but I am always talking about the human condition–
about what we can endure, dream, fail at, and survive.
—Maya Angelou

Start With Black Girls

(trace the path of braids)

BY PETER J. HARRIS

start with Black girls
stroke their daughterfaces
levitate when you hear them *and and and ...*
clap clap when you see them dance
study their jumprope choreography
listen when they open their minds
caress their hair even after bowing to the demands of discipline
pool their tears to irrigate sadness
chant the language of tomorrow as you rock baby to sleep

> *follow each purring strand out to*
> *nappy edges, baby hair & ungreased ends*
> *from 3 times tied to whiptip thin dangling, tucked or beaded*
> *a crown of tightly laced layers*
> *jewels upon handcrafted threads*
> *light skipping across precious stones*

if I was Peabo / or any singer in love
or any singer about love

I would swirl your name in my mouth before saying it
warm your name under my shirt before writing it
polish each word before telling friends & family my vows

part black hair
blow puffs of sweet breath
to seep almond oil into damp smiling after shampoo
tug & stroke shining furrows
squeeze a handful out of style
snake fingers within dark roots
sparks flash along braided patterns
halos inflame longwrapped twine in my glowing hands

your smells   your voices   extend my offshore waters
you tower in my sight like the ruins of Great Zimbabwe
your everpresence invisibly clouds my sight

bury my face into yielding entanglement   opened   caressed   home
wet fragrance brushes my closed eyelids

you walk into a room   I breathe through my eyes
you listen when I am all static
you massage my bruises with moody tales of watercolor adventures
you see our future when my imagination freezes over

I trace the path of braids
I tuck the burning between my fingers
I replant the heat in the twisted garden where it belongs

mango

BY XAVIA-MARGRITH MILES

In my palm ripened and full
reflecting all the sweetness Heaven and Earth could spare
I tenderly outline your shape

I'm in no hurry

Hasty eating pacifies hunger,
but for a moment
I aim for satiation

Before a taste
I surrender to your scent's embrace
Desire brews under my tongue
and I am consumed

Lips pressed against amber peel
and porcelain blades caress the flesh
Tongue twists & puckered pirouettes
leave golden pearls at the corners of my cheek
Unraveling is sweeter than I credit

Disclaimer: No mangoes were harmed in the making of this poem.

Dress Fabric of Faith

by Alprentice X Aries

I believe in the curve of her bonnet
The way it pulls out the devotion of my follow

I believe in the height of her sonnet
It tipped the Richter scale last month in San Francisco

I believe in the tint of her skin
The glow of off-brown tan and much-used cocoa butter

I believe in the sight of her sin
It's the reason the groundhog brings his ass out early

I believe in the bird that's so defiant
It rests and perches twice a day on unfamiliar electrical wires

Waiting

by Jennifer Maritza McCauley

I'm not ripe for mating, So
I carry myself well.

Underscored jaw,
Neck like lazy swan.
               (I'm joking. Not swan: jaunting cockatiel.)

I'm not really sure how you do it. Just being you:
which interminably is resplendent.

I know I've got it too: The beat and fast hips,
the wait and hide. I know the rituals to catch you:

And they bore me; you don't bore me.
Now here you are, laughing about some normal thing.

Here I go, gone. I bid you good luck. I love you alone,
now, then a bit later, in my room

             Where you can't see the extent.

The Commandment

by Thomasina Sanders

A simple commandment - never look back
A pact made one autumn afternoon
As leaves clung to various trees
And summer negotiated its final departure

Never challenging nor questioning this contract
Coordinating chance meetings on 38th street
Stepping quickly inside convenient doors
Always the Grand Hotel

Lobby allowing luscious greens
To play off deep mahogany wood
Marbled floors poorly absorb the click-clack of stilettos
While nomadic capitalists come and go

Near the window, I'd stand
Watching your reflection
Disregarding the regret or butterflies
In my stomach.

Planned inevitability came to pass.
Leaving the same we arrived
Calculated steps on cloud nine
Lost in languishing lust.

Dressed in only our afterglow, I looked back
Forsaking our only commandment
Instantly
I tasted the salt on my tongue

The Bed Isn't Made

by Ginger Galloway

The bed isn't made
Disheveled and upset— Looking like chitterlings.
I don't like them even wet with Louisiana Hot
The scent of your cologne
The pillows have the mark of hair grease and deodorant
Some decoration and some for sleep
My countenance tied up in the wrinkled sheets
Nothing about this bed is like it used to be
The creak of the box spring
The slant to one side
The place where my body lies
The parts of me thicker
Limbs that don't bend and twist
Heartbeats whose rhythm has lost their sync
And the bed isn't made
My countenance tied up in the wrinkled sheets
You pulled me close and
Told me how beautiful I look to you
Taking me wholly in big hands
Wrapped in the might of your arms
Pillows tossed on the floor
Kicking away damp covers
My countenance tied up in the wrinkled sheets

Back Then

by Thomasina Sanders

He remembers
The walks they used to take
Along Evans Street
In the shade of oak trees
Starting acorn and dirt rock fights
Building dams along curbs
To race crunchy autumn-tinted leaves
In the run-off from Mr. Martin's grass
Trickling down
His grandparents' peacefulness
Pooling in his recollection of harmony

She never forgets
How the smoke
From the chimney crawled easily
Down Evans Street on rainy, school day afternoons
To wrap its arms around her hesitancy
Comforting and beckoning her indecisiveness
To swing on rod iron gates
Laid masterfully between rectangular
Red earth-tinted bricks

He built ramps on Evans Street
To launch two-wheeled bicycles
And dreams into the stratosphere
While she gave dolls named Claudia and Sammy

Tea parties celebrating the arrival
That she would be more than just a girl

On Evans Street
MTV arrived
Atari's played Pac Man and Centipede
Sister Deon made Norman practice his tuba
While Nina's shouted "Ma'am" resonated
Off Mr. Jones '67 beige Chevy Impala
And life existed
Easily on Evans Street

Memory Paints

by Thomasina Sanders

I dipped my fingers in memory paints
Regressed back to my first childhood
Where simplicity existed
In a box of 8 different crayons
8 different ways to draw my world
8 different shades to produce a girl's
Struggle with her curiosity of life

I dipped my fingers in memory paints
To see if I still could make grass green
Red roses
Blue skies
And yellow suns shine

I dipped my fingers in memory paints
Allowed laughter to consume
Self-absorbent thoughts
As the speckled page
Comprised colorful characters
From my past

I dipped my fingers in memory paints
Drew two stick figures
Figuratively finding fondness
While watching whimsical wishes
Fly under rainbows
Taking dreams of our forever
To We Never Should Have Land

I dipped my fingers in memory paints
One last time
Just to feel what once was.
Then I washed my hands
Of us

'Til Death Do us Part

by Ahliah D. Sharp

My wedding day was full of happiness and tears as we vowed to love
each other.
For richer or poorer, in good times and bad, sickness and health,
'til death do us part.

'til DEATH do us part.

I always thought that meant someone has to die,
but… in a world where more than half of all marriages end in divorce,
I never stopped to think what *death* really means.

Divorce IS death!

It's final…it's devastating… It's…the end of what was and what will
never be again.
It's… solo dinners and, tear-soaked pillows..
It's…broken promises and dreams deferred….
It's…. the reality that happily ever after was a fairytale that failed…
It's…the last I love you … the last kiss
the last word ever spoken as the two of us became one return to two
alone once more…
It's…knowing that the Mr. and Mrs. went from hits to straight misses…
It's ….accepting that what was perfection is now complication…
It's… holidays split for the kids between households…
It's… sweetness turned bitter…
It's…. Death and
When I said I do, I thought someone would leave in a casket,

instead I was left feeling like a has-been.
'Ttil death do us part, is a crazy way to start
all over as another story unfolds.
Next chapter —singleness.
Sometimes a gift – sometimes a curse.
A time to heal pain and mend hurts.
It's time to be whole and get back control
of what I surrendered
when our vows turned to missed goals.
Lord knows life after divorce ain't no joke ...
It's ok to not be okay with the current status quo.
Embracing this journey does not make me weak,
loving myself fully is all that matters,
grace and self-affirmation,
understanding what went wrong,
and becoming everything that is meant for me to be.
Empowered in knowing that wholeness
in unconditional love is all I seek.

The Costco Kid

by EJ Jones

Four rooms, two baths, plus a detached garage, minus one son don't equal a home. I'd awakened with this fact, just me and my anger. The walls, ceiling, and floor were obviously too expensive to throw away, but it wasn't much more, not now. Reassurance from friends only irritated me, "Don't take it so hard. Just life right, but you got this place." And yeah, I owned a house, whooptyfuckingdo. I'd owned my anger decades longer; there was no question about my preference. But I'd ascended to a comfortable life and the routines of it already wore me like gloves. I did the things that people do in a house: admired my lawn over coffee and then ranted about the morning's news while on the toilet. The day dipped to worse when I noticed I held 5 sheets of toilet paper in my hand, having just finished what was definitely at least a 12-sheet shit. It was time to go to Costco. And luckily, I wasn't out of paper towels.

But the truth is, I don't like who I am in Costco. Most people there look either hopelessly lost or completely found. Having just lost someone precious, I didn't know if I had the bank account or stomach for that kind of experience. I knew I'd become a vacuum with a credit card and short-term memory. Of course, an 85-inch TV will improve the quality of a Laker's loss. Why wouldn't it? What if I am a caveman? I mean, it may seem excessive but where else can a disregarded man buy a gallon of Bourbon and Spicy mustard for the 40-pack of hot links in the fridge? All are badly needed, all fully stocked at Costco. I grabbed my headphones and hopped in the car, determined to let fury determine the speed and frustration guide the path.

To covet is to misplace anger, or at least it is for me, and I needed someone to blame for the emptiness in the house, in my life. I felt myself frown once I'd shown my card for entrance into the cathedral: fathers tussling hair on heads that came up to their waists, mothers raising babies in the air, kissing foreheads. I scrolled to a Wu-Tang playlist and tapped shuffle. "Cash Rules Everything around me, Cream...." Perfect, I thought, putting my head down and snagging a cart.

By the time I'd worked my way back to the frozen foods and alcohol, my cart was half full. I couldn't erase that I was indecipherable from everyone else, reaching and grabbing for momentary happiness, not need or utility. Glass food containers, sure. Plastic is cheap and ugly. A designer colander so I could feel like Emeril when I make my street famous spaghetti. Bam, Black olives. Bam, ground turkey. A little splash of Tabasco, Bam, Bam! Trash bags, too. Some Dog Food. A bottle of vino with an artsy label, so I could feel cultured and abandoned.

That's when I saw The Costco Kid. He was rail skinny, standing at the end of frozen foods, next to the cheese fridge wearing a too-small Yu-Gi-Oh shirt, staring directly right at me. By then I'd moved on to Method Man and was enjoying Bring the Pain a little too much to deal with someone else's kid. I thrust my chin in the air to acknowledge him and veered left. The Costco Kid followed. I gave a thin-lipped smile and dipped right. He mirrored me. Damn. I slid the music from my ears and took this kid in. He seemed middle class yet disheveled. He had on an oddly misaligned belt, freshly wiped tears under his glasses, and a thin line of snot coming out of his left nostril. The glasses were new but had been taped and retaped at the weakest parts of the frame. This was punishment for not taking care of something that takes care of your eyesight: embarrassment. I had one of those mothers. Wait, was I one of those fathers? A sharp dart hit me from nowhere. I thought of my own son, younger, darker, and now out-of-state; I reached for my headphones, but the Costco Kid reached for my hand.

"Please," the kid yelped, "You gotta help me." His voice spoke his true age, years less than his physical development. I wondered why this kid locked eyes with me rather than the 50 or so other people around us, people who could already hear him. The father in me kicked in, and I let myself be pulled to a large cardboard vat of bananas 20 feet away. For a moment, I stood there with him, confused, halfway thinking, is this little motherfucker trying to be funny dragging me to the banana box.

But the Costco Kid was sincerely frightened. "Mom said Bananas," he let slip, and the concern in his voice said he had an impatient mother. Again, I sympathized. He turned to look up at me, "But," he added with confusion, "No Bruises." I imagined he'd heard the word bananas and ran, not understanding he hadn't understood until he was halfway and was now afraid to go back empty-handed. Afraid to make a wrong decision, but equally afraid to make any decision, he'd chosen me, the angry black guy with headphones; he was oblivious to the customs of his own tribe and instinctively knew one of his own, me, a fellow oddball he could trust in a storm. I felt like a person, a father, for the first time since my home had become a house. And all of a sudden, I would have flown to South America with the Costco Kid, first class, to pick the perfect, ripest, and yellowest bananas on the continent.

I grabbed a bunch and put them in his hand, then snatched another bruised batch in mine. I pointed to the spots. "Bruises," I told him with a smile. His head swiveled from each hand for a moment. His long sigh and wide smile told me he now understood, but I wasn't expecting or ready for the hug. He leaped into my arms and held on longer than most people probably would have. The kid had bad breath and smelled like yesterday's dirt; I understood his mother's impatience. "You saved my life," he said, before trotting off with an arm full of Chiquitas.

One of the only personal beliefs I hold is a string of five words from a movie I love, "the sound part comes first," meaning that when you experience truth it comes to you in sounds, not words, and wisdom is acquired by learning to listen. Hearing the squeak and pop of this kid's footfalls, I felt enormous gratitude. Grateful that I had a mother whose patience wore thin with her son's forgetfulness, so much so that he learned to remember, sometimes the hard way, but he learned. I was comforted that I lived a life that allowed me to schedule runs and walks to sunsets and sunrises. I felt honored that I'd made a genuine stab at love and lost. And the sadness that had weighed me down for weeks lifted just enough that I could feel pride that my son had chosen to live with his mother because he wanted to help take care of her, even if it meant leaving his father alone. The scamper of the Costco Kid was more than music; the sound rose, spread throughout that cathedral, and I enjoyed every moment before it faded away. I wouldn't need my headphones for a while. I thought of the pride he'd have confidently showing his mother unbruised bananas, and the soft, approving smile I hoped she'd offer in return and began thinking that maybe home was made of materials, but materials with personalities. That could be it, just a place to hide, somewhere to pray or beat the walls when the world grows too scary.

I soaked up the moment too long, and couldn't find him or his mother when I reached the registers. But, before I left, I went back, back to the spot where I'd helped the Costco Kid, and picked up what I hoped were the same bruised bananas. Ain't gotta be perfect. Home, even mine, could be the same. The comfort of this possibility was enough to get me through the day, and when I hit the parking lot, I picked up speed, jumping on the hind legs of my cart to ride. Irritated shoppers and their kids didn't like some 40-year-old zipping past them shouting, "WU Tang," "WU-Tang," but it didn't matter by then. I was beginning to understand there was a way to be open to the world, a way that bred optimism. I listened to the wind whip past my ears and felt the rumble of the cart's wheels but still heard the music of the Costco Kid. After that, I went home, and realized once I got there, that I'd completely fucking forgotten the toilet paper.

Overtime Ghazal

BY ERIC DEVAUGHNN

on a thursday, when my bones could hardly ache more, my second job
asks me to work overtime,

although, I'm already fifty hours into a sixty-hour week. I've been ac-
cepting as much overtime

as the law will allow. my weekend shift stretches&extends into what
little remains of my life,

now that summer has released students&teachers alike—the year's
grind, over. time

to make plans, drive up the coast, lounge on lazy sand, pacific
beach&blue, until the season

shifts her tone, calls everyone back to task, to settle into the steady
crumble over time.

but today, an extra thirty minutes won't hurt. I suppose seven-&-a-
half dollars add up—perhaps

reason enough for some to stay—but my mind sneaks beyond the
walls, peers back over time

to revisit walking through my dark blue door, house pulsing with tiny
giggles&"Daddy's Home!"

&I could not be persuaded to offer up my body for more bruising
&choose money over time

with her. still, all good things must answer to their cost. the baby does
not know how infrequent

she is home, how painful the smiles play. this gutting game has not
ended, merely begun overtime.

my mind slinks back, ashamed for having failed to retain the only
 thing of any value. whispers,
"she is gone. there is nothing left but a schedule scribbled in dust." &I
 swallow hard, spill sorrow ovetime

lost. &worse—what refuses to gentle my heaving—I can hardly recall
 what so impressed upon us
each, that we could not set it aside. all that remains is the bitter break
 of war, now waged over time.

there are still things to live for. perhaps reason enough. but for the
 next twenty-eight minutes, I will focus
on the seven-fifty my ache is worth& hope hard work is somehow
 the key to pain fading over time.

ERIC DEVAUGHNN

In Your Room

BY DEVIN L. MITCHELL

Dad...
Since you've been gone
I have slept in your bed
The covers never reach my feet
And the night's always cold

Every morning I wake up
I hear the front door creak
The dogs moan in curiosity
They believe you're coming in

But it's the morning draft
Opening the door

The house feels bare without
But I feel your spirit
In your room...

New Blades Cry for A Slow Bloodletting

shaving as therapy & self-care an act of war

BY ERIC DEVAUGHNN

my father is no teaching man &so I did not learn to shave from
  him—although,

he may have shown me once, if quick, before I could grow hair
  enough to bring to blade.

now, peering back from beyond the grayed &spittle-splattered sink,
  my father's eyes

(clouded rosy-vein& vacancy) measure me, cheekbone-to-chin. we
  smile

&cupped warm water pools in collarbone&cleft. today, the steam is
  slow, the rinse

is cool, the lather extra thick &each deliberate&practiced pull
  demands

another pore mimic a battlefield—so careful cleared of carnage& the
  burned.

restored, the land declares her victory. &yet the war is waging on
  &still

the war, it wages on &yet (though war is waged on us, still) this war,
  we wage

Washing Collard Greens

by Beverly Head

"Come here! Hurry up!" My mother yells from the kitchen. I'm on my bed reading. I don't want to be disturbed.

"I know you hear me! Come here!" She yells again. I close my book and go to the kitchen.

"What?" I say, agitated because she has taken me away from my book. She is standing by the kitchen door holding one hand to her chest and pointing at the sink with the other hand. Her head is turned away from me.

"Get it out of the sink," she says.

When I look into the double sink, I see only collard greens floating in the water on one side and nothing on the other side.

"Get what?" I ask although I know why she has called me.

"Get that worm!" she hisses, getting mad at me because she knows I'm just being stubborn.

"I don't see a worm," I say because I want to fix her for making me put my book down. She rolls her eyes at me, and I know she is planning to come up with some way to punish me later, so I stick my hands into the water and pull up collard leaves. As the water drips back down, I scan for worms. Finally, I see a tiny white one who looks dead.

"Do you mean this little thing?"

"I don't care how little it is. Just throw it away or rinse it down the sink. Then finish picking and washing those collard greens because I can't stand seeing another worm today." After I pry the worm from the leaf, I thump it into the trash can. My mother jumps back although she is nowhere near the trash can. I grumble as I pick up each collard leaf, look at it carefully on both sides, and then throw it into the other sink. I can't believe that I have had to stop reading to pick and wash collard greens. My mother sits at the kitchen table and begins picking the peas that our neighbor has brought from a farm in the country. Thank God! I think. Peas don't have worms. When I finish, I let out a sigh as if I have been picking and washing collard greens for days. My mother ignores me, takes out cigarettes and matches, and sits holding them in her hand.

"I guess if you're going to start smoking, I'm gone. I was about to help you pick those peas, but I'm not breathing secondhand smoke." Of course, I had no plans to help pick the peas. I just want to irritate her about smoking. She doesn't say anything. Finally, she takes out a cigarette, lights it, and starts smoking. She drops the match into a plate of spaghetti left over from lunch. Soon she is tapping ashes on top of the spaghetti as well. I start waving cigarette smoke away from my face. She still ignores me. She keeps tapping ashes onto the food. It looks disgusting. Ashes soon cover the dried-up sauce and pale gooey noodles. I start to say that the noodles look like worms, but I don't. I wonder how she can sit and look at something so nasty. Finally, I give up trying to bother her about the smoking and the ash tapping. When I leave the kitchen, she is still smoking and tapping ashes. She looks tired. Her hair is still in pink foam rollers. They have been in her hair for almost a week. Each day she puts the same green scarf over them and goes about her routine. Her black and orange house coat is faded and raggedy around the hem. Scuffed-up shoes cover her dry, ashy feet. I feel a moment of pity. She is starting to look sad like my grandmother did before she left to live with my uncle in Cincinnati. My grandmother is scared of worms and snakes. Almost broke her neck one day jumping off the front porch steps because she thought my jump rope was a snake.

"Why are you so scared of worms?" I ask my mother when I return to the kitchen to get a root beer. She is still sitting at the table.

"Don't start asking me a lot of questions. I don't feel like answering them."

"I only asked one question."

"Well, I have one answer. I'm scared of them. Your grandmother and your aunts are scared of them. I guess your grandmother passed that fear down to all of us." "Well, it didn't get passed down to me. You ought to be glad of that. I guess those collard greens wouldn't have gotten picked and washed today if I had inherited that jumping around over little worms."

"I guess not."

She looks at me. "Thanks for finishing up the collards."

"You're welcome. Just don't call me anymore. I'm trying to read."

She ignores me and lights another cigarette. I am about to complain, but I don't. I go back to my bedroom. Later when I look in the kitchen after I finish reading my book, she is still sitting at the kitchen table, smoking, and putting out cigarettes in the leftover spaghetti. She looks up when I walk in but then looks back down. I don't ask any questions or complaints about the cigarettes and the ashes. Without being asked to, I put water in the pressure cooker and begin putting the collard greens in to cook for dinner.

Second-Hand Smoke

by BEVERLY HEAD

What would you say now
If we told you what your secondhand smoke
Has done to us

What would you say
About having your daughter's breast marked with a green pen so the
    surgeon would
know where to cut the cancer out

What would you say now
About my colon lined with precancerous polyps
Waiting to explode like little detonators

When we were young
you smoked and blew your smoke
into our faces at the kitchen table

although we begged you not to smoke
while we ate dinner

We did not know the dangers of secondhand smoke

House For Sale

by Beverly Head

Mama died
In the bedroom.
Daddy died
At the Kitchen table
With Johnnie Walker
And Jim Beam.
Sons and daughters
Escaped from the house
Leaving spirits to roam
From room to room
Unafraid of raw onions
Burnt on the stove
Undeterred by bottles
Filled with their names and
Buried deep in the backyard.

Singapore Slinging

by Judy Belk

Drunk, angry, sobbing, nursing a bruised cheek, and sprawled at the bottom of a very narrow closet with my newly purchased Fall wardrobe crumpled on top of me. Not exactly where I expected to be on the morning after my 18th birthday.

Just hours earlier, I was bar hopping in Georgetown thrilled to be the guest of honor as I celebrated what was an eagerly anticipated rite of passage in my Northern Virginia high school social network. Turn 18 and head to DC, which had a lower legal drinking age than my home state which required you to be 21.

Virginia has historically regulated alcohol like it's a horny virgin. It literally keeps hard liquor under lock and key—only sold in state-run Alcohol Beverage Control stores (aka ABC stores). So, I grew up thinking there was something mysterious and naughty about alcohol, which just added to the anticipation of turning 18 and sneaking across the Potomac to get a taste of the forbidden hard stuff. Prior to that, I had only dabbled.

My mom, a strong badass black woman, was a big beer drinker so occasionally I took the liberty of helping myself to her unfinished cans until she caught me one day and decided to teach me a lesson. The next time I took a sip, I got a mouth full of cigarette butts. She started using her beer cans as ashtrays and I quickly lost interest.

But as my 18th birthday approached, I started fantasizing about the art of drinking. Perched on a bar stool, holding a martini-like glass, sipping, looking sophisticated like a disinterested woman character from one of my favorite movies.

On my big day, I left the house early, dressed in a short clingy dress with lips glossed to the max. Since in my youthful mind turning eighteen also signaled that I was a true adult, able to come and go as I pleased, I intentionally didn't share my plans as I jumped in a friend's car and headed for DC.

I had always assumed that the first drink I would order would be a martini, but my friend persuaded me to try the syrupy sweet Singapore Sling---pineapple juice, triple sec, gin, and a cute little umbrella perched on a cherry. It would do in feeding my fantasy. So, it became my drink of choice for the evening. Five bars later and probably just as many Singapore Slings, the next thing I remember was sitting on the front steps of my house, shoes off, and not quite sure how I got there. The door was locked, and I didn't have a key. I started banging hoping to wake a sibling, even my father. Anyone except my mother who opened the door.

"Where the hell have you been? Do you know what time it is?" My mother's loud voice was vibrating off my aching head.

I stumbled past her with my shoes in hand. She followed.

"Did you hear me? Don't think you can walk in here anytime you want."

By this time, I had made it to my room and just wanted to go to bed. I was standing in front of my closet trying to get undressed and trying to remember how I got home from Georgetown.

"I'm going to ask you one more time. Where have you been?" She moved in closer to get a sniff. "You smell like alcohol. Have you been drinking? Where have you been?"

I was tired, drunk, 18, and unwise so I turned around and looked at my mother. I think I might have even tried putting my hands on my hips. But I was having trouble finding my hips as I responded with slurred confidence.

"Yes. I have been drinking. In case you haven't noticed, I am now 18. I'm an adult and I don't have to get your permission anymore if I want to go."

Before I could say the word, "out", the force of my mother's hand across my face propelled my unsteady half-dressed self back in the closet. I lost my balance, pulling, hanging clothes and the wooden rod with me as I hit the floor.

As usual, my mother had the last word.

"Have you lost your mind? Now get up and clean up that mess. Your birthday card is on the dining room table."

I squinted as the first glimmer of sunlight surfaced. The alcohol was wearing off

Making Piece

by Camryn Stevens

Jalissa didn't go out often, but tonight was special. She wanted to spend the most important birthday of her twenties doing something she loved something that always seemed to re-center her, something she hadn't been able to do for almost five months since the incident.

Most people Jalissa knew would want to spend their 21st birthday at a bar or a club with friends; and in the past, her birthday was a time to reminisce with old friends and laugh with new ones. But this was a night Jalissa wanted to herself, a chance to show gratitude to her body and make peace with her fears.

Around 7 pm, Jalissa left her house, roller skates tied together and hanging off one shoulder, her heavy, long-handled purse hanging over the other. She walked from her place to the skating rink as she'd done hundreds of times. She took the same shortcuts as she did before; she crossed through the parking lot of Big Al's to get to 8th Street, Jay walked when she hit Rancho Ave to avoid the barking of the four Dobermans that protected Mr. Reedley's yard, and finally, after passing the thrift store on Maple St., arrived at the back entrance of Lucky Leon's Skating Rink. Lucky Leon's was one of the oldest buildings in the neighborhood, and their competitive skating teams, along with their roller derby league, were their primary sources of income. Their next was Lucky Leon's Saturday Skate Night, which this year fell on Jalissa's birthday.

She walked up to the back door and knocked three times. When it opened, she was greeted by the surprised face of Luca, one of Rink 39's security guards and nephew of the current owner, Leon Jr.

"Jay! Wow! Hey, happy birthday! It's great to see you, you're back walking already?" Luca said, almost out of breath. Before she could respond, he looked at her skates. "Hey, you're not thinking about skating tonight, are you? You don't think that maybe," he paused, shifting his weight from one foot to the other before continuing, "maybe it's too soon?"

"Wow," Jalissa replied, ignoring his questions, "It's so good to see you too, *Lukie*!" She facetiously replied, calling him by his childhood nickname. With a tight smile and a voice sweeter than high fructose corn syrup she continued, "Yes, I'm having a *wonderful* 21st birthday, thanks for asking! I'm *sooo* excited, just *stoked*, to be celebrating at the rink tonight! It's just been *tooo* long." Tilting her head to the side and clasping her hands together, she peered up at him through her full lashes. "Can you make sure my song requests go to the top of the queue tonight?"

Arms crossed at his chest, Luca shook his head and smirked. "Yeah, okay Jalissa. I see you haven't lost your sense of humor."

Jalissa turned away and stifled a laugh into her shoulder. When she looked back she caught a look she'd never seen from the usually playful, laidback Luca.

"Hey, so," He cleared his throat and lifted the faded green baseball cap he always wore to scratch the dirty-blond curls underneath. The movement made the once holographic four-leaf clover logo dance before he fixed it back on his head. "Do they have any leads on the guy?" Luca asked in a softer tone.

Jalissa took a deep breath, releasing all the air before looking away again. From where they were standing in the back hallway, past the mops and the floor cleaning machine, and out the hallway door, she could see the skate floor, illuminated by a disco ball and overhanging lights. She looked to the DJ booth, then to the tables where all the non-skaters sat, and finally the snack bar area. She thought about all the years she had been coming to Lucky Leon's. She grew up here, skating with Luca, his siblings, and other childhood friends. Jalissa reminisced on the days when she first joined the youth skate team, a second grader, not yet old enough to walk to the rink by herself. Back then, her parents would make her older siblings walk her there, then eventually drive her once they got their licenses. Tyla, her older sibling, was now across the country in grad school, and though her second oldest sibling, Raheem, was only a forty-five-minute drive away, he was married and starting a family of his own. Tyla at age thirteen was already on the most advanced Gold Team by the time Jalissa was putting on skates for the first time at age five. They were one of the most graceful figure skaters Jalissa'd ever seen. Raheem on the other hand, about nine at this time, decided he preferred activities where his feet landed on solid ground. Still, he knew his way around the rink, and they all enjoyed leisurely skating together. Now they'd only go to the rink together if they could sneak off at some point during the holidays if everyone was back home.

With a quick shake of her head, Jalissa was pulled out of her memories and snapped back into the present moment. She looked at Luca and gave him a little smirk, taking in his freckled face and worried eyes. He was wearing typical Luca attire; distressed Vans, dark cargo pants, and an oversized forest green long-sleeve. "You know Luca, you could do without the old hat sometimes. You have really nice hair. You should let it breathe!" She said to him while backing out of the hallway. "But the color really does compliment your eyes!" Turning away from him, Jalissa hurried down the hallway. "I'll see you in the rink when your shift's over!" She called over her shoulder, and before he could stop her she was out the door.

As she strolled towards the main entrance on her way to the big entryway mirror, she passed the ever-growing crowd of skaters. People of all ages sat as they laced on their skates, or lined up at the snack bar, while others headed onto the rink. She scanned the crowd and smiled and nodded at familiar faces, careful to avoid conversations like the one she just had with Luca. She thought about what he said. *Do they have any leads on the guy?* She felt her stomach turn.

Relaxing her face into a smile, she approached the entryway mirror. Staring back at her was a thin-looking long-legged girl in a rhinestone-studded, fuchsia purple, long-sleeved velour zip-up hoodie, denim cut-offs, and flesh-colored, rhinestone-decorated fishnets. She pulled out her mahogany brown lip gloss that almost matched her complexion and reapplied. Though Jalissa had put a lot of effort into her birthday look this year, the way she had always done in the past, she couldn't help but feel like something was missing. She did a full face of makeup, even put on the jewelry she only wore for special occasions, and still couldn't shake the feeling that something was different. That she was different. Her curly afro, once thick and past her shoulders, was pulled into a slick low ponytail to hide the missing chunks. She brushed her hand across the stiff, gelled-down edges. It began to fall out the week she left the hospital and has been falling out ever since. Everything online said that the shedding would stop when her stress and anxiety levels returned to normal. In the meantime, she found that this hairstyle was the best way to conceal it. As she used a finger to plump up her mascara-coated lashes, she took notice of the dark bags that sat under her almond-shaped eyes and wondered if they'd ever go away.

Pulling away from the mirror, she stepped outside the front door for some fresh air. Sitting on the sidewalk, she took off her all-black platform Converse and began to loosen the glittery black laces on her hot pink skates. Looking around the surrounding neighborhood of Lucky Leon's, a barely audible gasp escaped her as she slowly stood up. Eyes squinted, she focused on the auto service and repairs shop across the street, and there, parked alone in the lot, she saw a familiar-looking SUV that sent chills down her spine.

Frozen, Jalissa felt an eternity pass. Her body broke into a sweat as the memories from that night rushed back. The image of a slow-moving, black Chevy Tahoe filled her mind. She remembered it being dark inside and smelling like motor oil and bleach. She remembered screaming so hard that she damaged her vocal cords and couldn't speak for two weeks, even after the shock wore off. And she vividly remembered the blood.

She didn't feel the bag slip off her arm, but she jumped when it hit the pavement. She looked down at the heavy leather purse and suddenly remembered why she carried it with her in the first place. She glanced back inside and scanned the area, taking in the laughter and smiles. Her eyes landed on Luca, and she watched as he whispered something to the DJ. A few seconds later the song cut from Party in the U.S.A. to Atomic Dog, and most everyone that wasn't already skating ran onto the rink. She wondered if he noticed she wasn't in the rink yet. She wondered if he would agree with what she was about to do. If, in her position, he'd do the same.

Wasting no time, she slipped back into her outdoor shoes and laced them up. Setting her skates on the inside of the door she closed her eyes and took a deep inhale and held. *You've imagined this exact moment a million times*, she said to herself. Releasing her breath and opening her eyes, she cautiously walked towards the car shop with her bag across her shoulder. As she got closer to the parking lot, she stopped and put her right hand inside the black bag, searching for the comfort of the cool metal she had become familiar with while in isolation for the past few months. She slid her finger around the trigger and took a deep breath as she moved toward the car. First, she peered in through the back window. Seeing nobody in the car, she slowly walked up the side and toward the entrance of the garage. The area was dark, and closed for the night. The only light came from the flickering streetlamp, and she could hear the bass from the skating rink's music across the street. *You could always turn back, a voice whispered in her head. Run away and make it, like last time.* Hesitating at the entrance of the open hanging doors, she started to back away. That's when she heard footsteps.

"Can I help you with something, Miss?"

She heard the gravelly voice she knew she could pick out if it was a whisper in a crowded school hallway. The voice of the one she couldn't let haunt her subconscious any longer.

Slowly, a tall, slender, scraggly-haired man appeared from the shadows of the open car garage, wiping his hands on a towel before tucking it into his pocket. Jalissa's stomach dropped to her knees and her mouth went dry. As he got closer and closer, her body began to tremble. For a moment, they were locked in a stare. Her fingertips caressed the smooth, cold instrument inside her bag. She couldn't quite read the expression on his face, but she didn't care to.

Gunshots. Warmth shocked her hand as her zip-up was tie-dyed red and her lips tasted like iron. A metallic scent rose in the air, lifted and carried by the summer breeze of the night.

The man that was once standing across from her a moment ago stumbled backward, shocked. There was a thud as he sank to his knees, then smacked face-first onto the ground. Eyes frozen open, his body lay still in a growing red puddle.

Head spinning, Jalissa turned mechanically and slowly walked back to the skating rink. She could feel the still-warm hole in her purse.

For the second time that night, she walked up to the back door, knocked three times, and waited.

THESE BLACK BODIES ARE
TRANSFORMING

All that you touch You Change.
All that you Change Changes you.
The only lasting truth Is Change."
— Octavia E. Butler

5th Street Sky

BY PETER J. HARRIS

for Richard Fulton

white clouds drift over a bandstand of raining sighs brighten after
    hours with storms proclaiming my my my steaming away wrin-
    kles in once sprawling lives

under the 5th Street sky

grown men cradle horns
float solos full of caffeine & whipped cream
sweeten melody with aroma of their high-hat wisdom return time's
    meaning for twitching family members once slumped on side-
    walks cackling with pain
now bowing into music with no shame

        ... sacred gone ground found ...
        summoning us into forgiveness
        praise of dishonored angels
        on the black & white walls

    beneath 5th Street Dick's baby blue ceiling

        we find shelter from sticks & stones
        bad days & broken bones
        bottles & bubbles
        sour drink & endless troubles

look how light falls on the humid faces turned up
as old timers tip toe into Harlem Dip & Central Avenue Stroll
stride past the curve of a sizzling piano

finger snaps shooting sparks through the air
old school medicine sipped & savored by hip-hop heads
igniting language incinerating diction like lindy hopping dragonflies
    homing in on a kaleidoscope of Monarch butterflies
to conjugate fantastic murals across the dazzling 5th Street sky

who remembers the dawn when our cherished OG waved goodbye?
I will never forget the dawn when our cherished OG waved goodbye

Since We Last Spoke

BY XAVIA-MARGRITH MILES

Disclaimer: The person in front of you is an experienced mischief seeker, attempt at your own risk.

1. Called my vice by its name   sensation.
2. With 4% phone battery, 3 lefts on unmarked roads, 2 rights where the wind was quiet, left one sufficiently lost and wandering creature.
3. Made my body an altar.
4. Asked children their superpower.
5. Made a bed in the wounds of a lover (I overstayed and left a salt bath behind).
6. Asked a lover how I wounded them and offered them a tangerine (to accompany my 9- tiered apology).
7. Befriended a tree.
8. Ate something that frightened, repulsed, compelled me (like red clay, or anything with raisins).
9. Asked birds and strangers to share their beauty secrets.
10. Reintroduced myself to home. Clicking my combat boots 3 times//before paying my greyhound fare// "the smoke meat not meth" sign still overlooks the butcher's// my mother still watches over the town's soul.
11. Embraced a chill for warmth, sometimes this means home too.
12. Smacked loudly with closed eyes on buttered bread to evenly distribute cream and crunch to all parts of mouth.
13. Climbed up a great-great-grand branch, in two-inch-junk-glittered acrylic talons-I'd never danced in midair but I have fallen. And a new word for terror and elation struck before I landed.

Whether these be offerings,
to satiate the lust of a trickster,
humor a god,
entertain the stars,
stories whistled from my porch when I am old,

May the places I am porous and wandering be evidence of life.

Amen

Walk

BY GERDA GOVINE ITUARTE

WALK

   SDRAWKCAB

      On

         crystal

           stairs

              in

                stiletto

                  heels

                    DEDLOFDNILB

Stillness

After Langston Hughes

BY JAMES COATS

Throw away the body.
This life absent frequent quiet
pauses in service to nothing.
Beyond a first doves flight
to question our peace.
Beyond a first rock's rise
to spill precious liquid.
When a first whole
is not yet whole, but empty
when the ending is not found
and here is also not now.
Solid and restricted self
gives way to forgotten knowing -
something immense is present.
Life isn't much quiet
much elusive quiet.
Silencing death
to Leave!
Leave!

In Memoriam

BY AKUA LEZLI HOPE

for poet Baron James Ashanti 1948-2018

even spring leaves fall
torn by angry gusts, huge hale
and late-arriving roses bloom
too quickly, fried by horrific heat
still there is green, the old apple tree flowers
just in time, tiny green fists defy many tragedies,
incursions by the wantonly hungry aiming high
el dia que me quieras pours from an unimagined
magic phone, version after version
collected over years, things we couldn't afford
and didn't need, working for our culture,
one enduring gift ————— Gato's urgent wail
leaps from that vinyl spinning above
the Brooklyn apartment's parquet floor
shimmers long-windowed Gowanus light
traced our gathering commitment
to transform longing into language, incantations
subtle insurrections opening third eyes,
programming progress, moving stone, unshackling
absence wars no more foxman, baron bunny,
wayward transmutations fly fly rocket inner outer
this decohering cri de coeur reminds
of what might have been
given what was taken lost what yet
yet yet remains

Alabama - Coltrane

by Camryn Stevens

Smoke caught in a distant breeze,
white flags raised,
the drums they beat and they played.
Lightening cracked its whip,
a saxophone loaded and gripped.
A guitar gently hummed,
broken back on the barrel of a gun.
Each teardrop was a prayer.
Black skin and braided lips
tied together for a kiss.
The final breath of defeat,
legs giving way to release.
Sturdy branches bloody leaves,
dangling from a willow tree.

Soul #2

by Richard May III

there will always be music

BY PAMELA PETÉ

NIGGER
            jerked my head up

every bellowed beat before
blurred background noise

his deep blue battered truck
a rumbling bass
head out window   hollering
hate   hanging spit on every syllable
singing fist   sparking fire

punching gas
screeching stop
punching gas

a once low tune   now louder
needle bumped   scratched   stuck
on baritone deep memories

skip repeat   skip

until the noise blends   droning
derogatory   distant yet drumming
band like blending   yet we all know him
the white hood of his heart

i hummed the hymn
my forefathers hummed
all of us holding harmony here
                              —this day

in my head   my heartbeat
beating hard beating fast
a jingling tambourine
                    —held tight

i knew the dragged retaliating rhythm
the song   lyrics of james byrd jr
emmett red trails   it's an old song

it's melody overpowering
my mind fills with black notes
swinging   from trees   screeching
of a soloist's soprano

flashes of floyd
breathing   breonna
flashes

and now this

he was leaving his parking spot
as i parked my presence
like my red mercedes   sleek   sober

i exit   bold and brazen
shoulders back   leading with chest
this battle isn't mine   in my mind

PAMELA PETÉ

there   on my neck   i could feel him
ignorant of my offense i tense
gearing up for a gun

never make eye contact
avoid confrontation
be black   ground   still
engrained melody

so i sing

regimen (for bessie)

BY JACQUESE ARMSTRONG

drums hued from sister
trees shout a joyous refrain
incandescent rays of Hope...

speak Love over yourself
daily
my auntie
it is your armor/your shield
a covering passed down from
conscious loving black hand to
conscious loving black hand
with a quick kiss hug before
leaving any outer doorway

this is our way.

we are the origin of the Wind
they know not where we come or go
we are the night cobalt/diamond stars
navigating liberty flight

so
shine your armor/your shield
carry centuries' love as clothing
speak that Love over yourself daily
as God makes the Sun to rise
a blossom orange overwhelming
maze.

there is promise in us
as we have been kissed by the Wind
at birth
magic words placed in our hearts
by ancestors
inspire wings.

so
if the day comes when
we find our cups not overflowing/
we see it as neither half empty
or half full
we
are simply grateful to hold the cup
and the Wind
remembering our promise
lifts us upward
and we fly...

...but now dear bessie
you've captured Promise
the Wind remembered you
you are free
and you fly

and we are reminded
to give thanks in every situation/
i
am thankful simply
that you were here to Love

Un Petite Morte in the key of "Here I Go" by Mystikal

BY XAVIA-MARGRITH MILES

Lay me in a bed of lavender,
lingerie on the outside, pearl daggers
joined to the bone in my hand
to open my letters, scratch my scalp, tickle birds.

Paint lips black as mud,
no, like blues.
Soul like mud,
sticky and whimsical.

It's a fish fry, but a roast
Make death a plate and let a laugh track play me off.
Tears are for the living-prayer
for the dead-water.

Tell of the debauchery and joy.

Don't make me no saint.

But momma might be there,
tell her I loved,
was loved

and will be loved deeper still.

For those that remain

BY XAVIA-MARGRITH MILES

Once held by ancestors and gods,
Bodies folded together like the pages of loved books
Kiss-sealed greetings and lingering departures,
have not warmed us for at least a gnat's ion.
40 years to the trees.

Bread and earth take 30 seconds to bake
and memories disappear in the same.

Currency of the Realm:
Shit is gold
Gold is gold
Oil is gold because it is fuel.
Water is life (when scarce, gold).

But parts of us remain:
Cecily Tyson, Twinkies, love, bullets, roaches, and fire.

We've always had fire.

Peace, light, and progress to the spirit of our beloved Mama Cecily

on the wings of angels: a chorus

in   the sky
the beginning there   like kin
like music   leaving
was   arms
us playing   fingers
keyboards   wanting
only   to fly
wanting   only breath
life   our skin
this is what   it means
to be alive

1- stay black
2- breath
3- know yourself as free

in the body's bones   it curls
hollow   and steps
wailing like   gasp like
loft music   an owning
of self
that starts   history
or time   where we know
ourselves   we made
time
new
suns
3 - trust this   our bodies crossed
4- home is here   oceans
5- grow

to eat   drink and catch
the stone   in the throat
how can you   now be ever be
so tired
when these   footprints
are   paths
of   queens
you   are
child   unfeathered
raise   the horns
unfurl   the wings

and find here a
little belief self
love sprinkled
on the floor petals and seeds
that braid themselves into your hair

or else find here the brown couch
waiting and blessing the coming

trumphets and horns

an arrival

a landing
an acceptance
plumed out

6 - like the past and the
now and the future is truly
ours again

NIKIA CHANEY

Acknowledgments

Armstrong, Jacques

"Will a Flower Bloom from a Multi-Tasking Pain?" was previously published in *Stellium a Literary Magazine* (now defunct).

"my hair is natural dammit (i can stand the rain)" was previously published in *Black Magnolias Literary Journal*.

"Regimen (for Bessie) an iteration" was previously published in *BLK Voices Magazine*.

Harris, Peter J.

"5th Street Sky" was previously published in *Brooklyn & Boyle*, East L.A. newspaper, 2022.

Head, Beverly V.

"Washing Collard Greens" was previously published in *Wildflower Magazine* in 2011.

Matthews, Fallen

"I am the Night Color Me Black: The Vampire Positionality of the Black Pedagogue in Ganga & Hess" was previously published in *Pivot: A Journal of Interdisciplinary Studies and Thought* 9(1) in October 2022.

Washington, Mitchell

"Melanin Canyon" was previously published in *Paradise Poems* in 2022.

I am the Night Color Me Black: The Vampire Positionality of the Black Pedagogue in Ganga & Hess By Fallen Matthews

Works Cited

Aksan, Cihan. "Revisiting Frantz Fanon's the Damned of the Earth: A Conversation with Lewis R. Gordon." Versobooks.com, New Left Review, 1 May 2018, https://www.versobooks.com/blogs/3775-revisiting-frantz-fanon-s-the-damned-of-the- earth-a-conversation-with-lewis-r-gordon.

"Equity, Diversity, Inclusion, and Accessibility." Centre for Learning and Teaching, Dalhousie University, https://www.dal.ca/dept/clt/edia.html.

Ganja & Hess. Directed by Bill Gunn, performances by Duane Jones and Marlene Clark, 1973.

Guerrero, Ed. "The Rise and Fall of Blaxploitation." The Wiley-Blackwell History of American Film, edited by Lucia, Cynthia, et al., vol. 3, ser. 60, Oxford University Press, 2012, pp. 1- 35.

Gunn, Bill, director. Ganja & Hess. Kelly-Jordan Enterprises, 1973.

Lawrence, Novotny. Blaxploitation Films of the 1970s: Blackness and Genre. Routledge, 2012.

Lykidis, Alex. "Black Representation in Independent Cinema: From Civil Rights to Black Power." The Wiley-Blackwell History of American Film, edited by Lucia, Cynthia, et al., vol. 3, ser. 55, Oxford University Press, 2012, pp. 1-16.

Quinn, Eithne. ""Tryin' to Get Over": Super Fly, Black Politics, and Post-Civil Rights Film

Enterprise." Cinema Journal, vol. 49 no. 2, 2010, pp. 86-105. Project MUSE, doi:10.1353/cj.0.0183.

Saucier, Jamie C. "Suburban Culture." The Oxford Encyclopedia of American Cultural and Intellectual History, edited by Rubin, Joan Shelley, and Scott E. Casper, vol. 2, Oxford University Press, Oxford, UK, 2013, pp. 453-459.

Terry, John Robert (2012). "Towards the Gendering of Blaxploitation and Black Power," Madison Historical Review, vol. 9, pp. 79-105.

Being Jean Toomer in America by Calvin Shaw

Works Cited

"Jean Toomer Biography." The Biography.com. Updated 3 November 2016. https://www.biography.com/people/jean-toomer-37322. Accessed 22 April 2018.

"Kenneth Rexroth." PoetryFoundation.org. https://www.poetryfoundation. org/poets/kenneth-rexroth. Accessed 22 April 2018.

Byrd, Rudolph P. & Gates Jr., Henry Louis. "Jean Toomer's Conflicted Racial Identity." Chronicle of Higher Education. Vol. 57 Issue 23, pB5-B8. 11 February 2011. Article.

Ramazani, Jahan. Ellmann, Richard. O'Clair, Robert. "Portrait in Georgia." The Norton Anthology of Modern and Contemporary Poetry. Vol. 1 Modern Poetry, 3rd Edition. W.W. Norton & Company, Inc. 500 Fifth Avenue, New York, NY. 10110. 2003. Print. Pg. 560.

Ramazani, Jahan. Ellmann, Richard. O'Clair, Robert. "Reapers." The Norton Anthology of Modern and Contemporary Poetry. Vol. 1 Modern Poetry, 3rd Edition. W.W. Norton & Company, Inc. 500 Fifth Avenue, New York, NY. 10110. 2003. Print. Pg. 559.

Authors & Artists

Maya Adenihun is a graduating senior at Los Osos High School and she has presented her poetry at the Segerstrom Center for the Arts Juneteenth Celebration. In the future, Maya hopes to be a sociologist, professor, writer, and artist.

My black body is **Precious.**

Alprentice X Aries is a writer and poet from Michigan. He has been published in several journals such as *Bangalore Review, Rigorous Magazine,* and *Black Sunflowers Poetry SMEOP* issue just to name a few. Alprentice is currently working on the final touches of his first volume of poetry and prose. Alprentice X Aries believes in freedom of mind, freedom of thought, and freedom of body for all.

My black body is **Victorious.**

Keisha-Gaye Anderson is a Jamaican-born poet, writer, visual artist, and media strategist based in Brooklyn, NY. She is the author of *Gathering the Waters* (Jamii Publishing 2014), *Everything Is Necessary* (Willow Books 2019), and *A Spell for Living* (Agape Editions), which received the Editors' Choice recognition for Agape's Numinous Orisons, Luminous Origin Literary Award. Keisha's poetry, fiction, and essays have been widely published in national literary journals, magazines, and anthologies. In 2018, Keisha was selected as a Brooklyn Public Library Artist in Residence. Keisha holds an M.F.A. in creative writing from The City College, CUNY. Learn more about her at www. keishagaye.ink.

My black body is **Stellar.**

Jacquese Armstrong, author of *birthing yourself naturally: motivational reflections on a mental health journey* (2022) and *blues legacy* (Broadside Lotus Press, 2019), was the recipient of the 2019 Naomi Long Madgett Poetry Award and 2015 Ambassador Award from the State of New Jersey Governor's Council on Mental Health Stigma for promoting wellness and recovery and reducing stigma through the arts.

My black body is **Eclectic.**

Nefertiti Asanti (@electricfl0wer) is a poet born and raised in the Bronx and recipient of fellowships and residencies from the Watering Hole, Lambda Literary, Anaphora Arts, Winter Tangerine, Museum of the African Diaspora, and PEN America. Nefertiti's debut chapbook *fist of wind* won the inaugural Start a Riot! Chapbook Prize. Their work can be found at Foglifter, Split Lip Magazine, Santa Fe Writer's Project, and elsewhere.

My black body is **Lore.**

Race, family, justice, and hope are constant themes in **Judy Belk's** writing which includes essays, poetry, and short stories. Her work has appeared in the *Los Angeles Times, New York Times, Washington Post, and National Public Radio,* as well as in *The Phoebe, Griffin, Wind* magazines. She has received two writing residencies at Hedgebrook, a mecca for women writers authoring change. A native of Alexandria, Virginia (before it was a tourist destination), she currently lives in Los Angeles.

My black body is **Fine.**

Denise T. Best is the president and CEO of the Voices of Women of Color, a social justice firm in Hartford, Connecticut. She is an educator and published writer who has performed in the Hartford area for more than 40 years as a vocalist, actor, and dancer. Denise has a smooth jazz radio show, Sunday Serenade, from 10 AM until noon, EST on primal4k.com.

My black body is **Regal.**

Stephani Maari Booker is surviving the fire, plague, and wrath of the 2020s in Minneapolis, MN. The author of *Secret Insurrection: Stories from a Novel of a Future Time,* her poetry has been published most recently in *St. Paul Almanac, Unfit to Print* and *Queer Voices: Poetry, Prose, and Pride.* For more information about her work, go to www.athenapersephoni.com.

My black body is **Mortal.**

Shonda Buchanan is the author of five books, including the award-winning memoir, *Black Indian*. She is a Pushcart Prize nominee, Oxfam Ambassador, USC Los Angeles Institute for the Humanities Fellow, and City of Los Angeles (COLA) Department of Cultural Affairs Master Artist Fellow, Senior Lecturer in the Department of African American Studies and Writing Instructor in First Year Seminar at Loyola Marymount University, Shonda is also a faculty member in Alma College's MFA Program in Creative Writing.

My black body is **the Ocean.**

Katerina Canyon is a Sunland-Tujunga Poet Laureate. She currently lives, writes, and teaches in Seattle, Washington.

My black body is **Restless.**

Kenny Carroll is a writer from DC. He was the 2017 DC Youth Poet Laureate, and in 2019 received the Thomas Lux Scholarship from Sarah Lawrence. His work has been featured in Split This Rock's *The Quarry*, *The Hill Rag*, and *Beltway Quarterly*, among others.

My black body is **Here.**

Nikia Chaney is a multi-genre author and artist. She has published two poetry books, *To Stir &* (Word Works, 2023) and *us mouth* (the University of Hell Press, 2018), a memoir, *Ladybug* (Inlandia, 2022), and a short volume of science fiction, *Three Walking* (Bamboo Dart Press, 2021). She teaches in Santa Cruz.

My black body is **Prism.**

Davian Chester is a creative from Georgia. He is best known for creating major social statements with his art. By Illustrating *These Black Bodies Are . . .* his work brings awareness and initiates discussions in the Black community.

*My black body i*s **History.**

Ashton Cynthia Clarke is an African American/Afro-Caribbean, Los Angeles-based writer, and storyteller. She has work published in *Spectrum 33: You and Me*; *The Storytelling Bistro: Stories, Poems, and Reflections*; *The Academy of the Heart and Mind*; and *Olney Magazine*. Ashton has performed her true, personal stories on stages throughout the L.A. area and New York City, as well as virtually.

My black body is **Legion.**

James Coats is an author, poet, and educator born in Los Angeles and raised in the Inland Empire. He believes that poetry has the ability to bring diverse groups together, offering a way to connect through shared challenges, achievements, and experiences. His newest poetry collection *Midnight & Mad Dreams* is published by World Stage Press.

My black body is **Fascinating.**

Cory Besskepp Cofer is the author of *Dreaming Under Polka-Dot Stars*, a collection of poems published by World Stage Press. An Educator for over 20 years, his distinct voice and lived experiences enrich the classroom in ways that can't be quantified. He is co-founder of A Mic & Dim Lights, a long-running poetry reading based out of Pomona, CA, that has cultivated a birthing ground for community building and collaboration for creatives locally and across the country.

My black body is **Cyclical.**

Naysha Coker is an adventurous writer looking to share the stories of life's journeys, in verse. In recent years she graduated (December 2022) with a bachelor's in Sociology from Cal State University San Bernardino. Whenever she decides to put pen to paper, she starts with a prayer.

My black body is **Beautiful.**

Klarissa Conner is an up-and-coming writer from Ontario California. She is obtaining her bachelor's degree at the California State University of San Bernardino as an English Major with a Creative Writing concentration. You can find more of her work in the literary magazine, Poems of Unique Experiences-Pacific Review.

My black body is **Courageous.**

Lynda V. E. Crawford was born and raised in Barbados and lives in the United States. Both homes sway and punctuate her writing. Lynda writes to sneak behind eyes, blow through ears, and stretch voices. Her poems have appeared in print and online journals and anthologies including *ArtsEtc Barbados*, *The Caribbean Writer*, *The Galway Review*, *The Bookends Review*, and *Exposition Review*.

My black body is **Ancestral.**

Eric DeVaughnn is a father, author, educator, and poet. He teaches elementary physical education in San Bernardino, California, where he resides. All his poems are cracked teeth, dusky yellow, and receding gum lines lying limp on waxy, bright white paper, speckled red.

My black body is **Deafening.**

Denise R. Ervin is a creative writer hewn from the streets, classrooms, and boardrooms of Detroit. She has spent two decades performing poetry and leading workshops for Midnight & Indigo and Room Project. Her work has been published or is forthcoming in *AADUNA, Third Wednesday Magazine,* and others and, most recently, she was selected as a Writing Fellow by The Watering Hole and a semifinalist for *America's Next Great Author.*

My black body is **Compromised.**

Veronica Evans is a long-time Nichiren Buddhist, philosopher, public speaker, and writer focused on exploring the interconnectedness between people and their intimate environments. As a Midwest transplant, she continues to seek tangible opportunities to develop her humanity without boundaries and contribute to American society.

My black body is **Eternal.**

Angela M. Franklin is an essayist, poet, visual artist, and documentarian. She holds an MFA from Antioch University Los Angeles. She writes across genres and enjoys crafting prose poetry and writing memoirs that capture and reflect the Black experience.

My black body is **Resolute.**

Karen Frederick is an avid reader, runner, and teacher. She divides her time between Los Angeles and Washington, DC. Her stories have appeared in *Scriblerus, The Paragon Press, The Evening Street Review, Underwood, Moonlight and Indigo, Inlandia,* and the *Book Smugglers Den.*

My black body is **Magnificent.**

There is a therapy in the keys of the computer, a tippy-tapping voice of reason and solace that no degree prepares the heart for. **Ginger M. Galloway** is a wife and mother of 7, and Gigi to 3 beautiful grandsons. Author, Poet, and Playwright, Ginger is a graphic designer and artist. She earned her BA in Human Development from Azusa Pacific University and has taught in the arts and academia inspiring young children. Her published credits include two novellas, *Destiny Interrupted* and *Hope for Lunar Days*, two picture storybooks, *Gerald Learned to Tie His Shoes* and *What I Really Want to Be*, collections of poetry and inclusion in a number of anthologies. As a side gig, Ginger sews dolls and plays with yarn, wood, and paint.

My black body is **Creative.**

April Gardner is a Christian, daughter, sister, niece, aunt, and educator. A life motto she has witnessed and continues to witness, in her family is," Do your work as unto the Lord." She strives to continue to perpetuate this motto in all the work that she does.

My black body is **Bold.**

After years of working for media, higher education, and non-profit organizations, **Elizabeth Gibbs** is 'free-tired' and pursuing her passions of writing, teaching, and leading workshops on self-awareness. She is an award-winning author, writes for several health and wellness blogs, and has published three books, *Soul Food, Enlighten Up!* and *Ogi Bogi, The Elephant Yogi*, a children's book. Her personal blog can be found at https://www.bethgibbs.com

My black body is **Connected.**

Natalie J. Graham is an award-winning author and performer who has toured nationally with her collection of poems, *Begin with a Failed Body*. In August 2021, Natalie was appointed Poet Laureate of Orange County. A widely published scholar with research interests in race, identity performance, and music, she is also a professor in the Department of African American Studies at Cal State University.

My black body is **Delicate.**

Chris "The Poetic Genius" Green is a poet from Gloucester, Virginia writing with the hopes to live up to his moniker "The Poetic Genius." Chris recently won the Poetry Society of Virginia's Honoring Fatherhood award for his poem "Breaking Myth", a poem about the misconceptions about black fathers. Chris "The Poetic Genius" Green hopes that his poetry will honor his people and inspire many including his singer/songwriter 7-year-old daughter Layla.

My black body is **Valuable.**

George Hammons is a California native, who spent his childhood in Phoenix, Arizona. George moved to Compton, California as a teen and graduated from Verbum Dei High in Watts. George studied creative writing at California State University San Bernardino. George attributes his love and pursuit of poetry to writers, such as Gwendolyn Brooks, Gil Scott-Heron, Paul Laurence Dunbar, Langston Hughes, Elizabeth Bishop, Shakespeare, and Mouhamed Ali as well as the many voices and personalities he encounters when interacting with everyday people.

My black body is **Creative.**

Peter J. Harris, Altadena Poet Laureate Editor in Chief (2022-2024), is the author of *Safe Arms: 20 Love & Erotic Poems (w/an Ooh Baby Baby moan)*, with Spanish translations by Francisco Letelier (FlowerSong Press), and *Song Again* (Beyond Baroque Books). In 2015, his book of poetry, Bless the Ashes (Tia Chucha Press), won the PEN Oakland Josephine Miles Award, and his book of personal essays, The Black Man of Happiness: In Pursuit of My 'Unalienable Right,' won the American Book Award. Harris is the founding director of The Black Man of Happiness Project, a creative, intellectual, and artistic exploration of Black men and joy. He writes the blog *WREAKING HAPPINESS: A Joyful Living Journal:* www.inspirationcrib.com

My black body is **Mine.**

Danielle Hayden is a Seattle-based writer who grew up in Detroit. She is currently at work on a novella and an essay collection.

My black body is **Free.**

Beverly V. Head taught College Level English for 38 years. Her book of poetry, *Walking North*, published by Michigan State University Press as part of the Lotus Poetry Series, was the second winner of the Naomi Long Madgett Poetry Award.

My black body is **Sassy.**

Michael G. Hickey (Gloria Smith) shared two of her personal narratives with her partner, Michael, who wrote them down furiously. Gloria and Michael live in Seattle and have been together since 11/11/18.

My black body is **Sacred.**

Akua Lezli Hope, 2022 Grand Master of Fantastic Poetry (SFPA), is a paraplegic creator & wisdom seeker who has been in print since 1974 with over 450 poems published. Her collections include *Embouchure: Poems on Jazz and Other Music* (Writer's Digest book award winner), *Them Gone, & Otherwheres: Speculative Poetry* (2021 Elgin Award winner). A Cave Canem fellow, her honors include the National Endowment for the Arts, two New York Foundation for the Arts and NYSCA fellowships, a Science Fiction and Fantasy Poetry Association award, & multiple Best of the Net, Rhysling & Pushcart Prize nominations.

My black body is **Cherished.**

Dr. Gerda Govine Ituarte published five poetry collections from 2012-2023. Her memoir is a work in progress.

My black body is **Full of Grace.**

Dion Jahmal is a poet and author. His poems, sonnets, and Blāküs have been published in various anthologies, including Poetry Soup and Parkland Poets. His unapologetic approach to poetry is the result of over fifty winters spent as a multi-cultured human in this experiment called America.

My black body is **Glorious.**

EJ Jones graduated from UC Riverside with a Bachelor of English and a Master of Fine Arts. He currently teaches at San Bernardino Valley College.

My black body is **Fluid and Impermanent.**

Shirley Jones Luke is a poet and writer. Ms. Luke lives in Boston; Mass. Shirley is working on a poetry collection.

My black body is **Defiant.**

Judy Juanita's *The High Price of Freeways* won the 2021 Tartt Fiction Award [Livingston Press, 2022]. *Manhattan my ass, you're in Oakland,* her poetry collection [Equidistance Press], was awarded the Before Columbus Foundation's American Book Award for 2021.

My black body is **Triple-hearted.**

Born in Trenton, New Jersey, **Duan Kellum** came to California at the age of 3. He is an educator, artist, and activist. Kellum's predominant medium is screen printing with an interest in stenciling. He first entered the art scene in 2003 with a graphic t-shirt called, "Freedom is Slavery". The design was based on a passage from the George Orwell classic, 1984. The primary focus of his works consists of social, environmental, and political themes. His works tend to utilize familiar iconic pop motifs and images. Current work includes abstract designs and stenciling. He has participated in many group shows and exhibits. Many of his prints can be found at the Center for the Study of Political Graphics (Los Angeles), Interference Archive (New York), Artlands (Redlands) He is the editor of *LOUD: Politics of Art & Art of Politics* and is the co-owner of Creative Grounds Art Studio in San Bernardino, Ca. Kellum currently lives and works in Southern California.

My black body is **Funny, Adventurous, and Generous.**

Vicki Lee is a lifelong resident of San Bernardino, California, and an active member of New Hope Missionary Baptist Church. She is a community activist and advocates for those in need. Her ultimate goal is to let her light shine for Christ.

My black body is **Grateful.**

Stephanie Liggins is an anointed child of God, a wife, mother, and grandmother. After a 30-year career as a teacher, she is presently a seminarian majoring in Christian counseling.

My black body is **Blessed.**

Sheila Marchbanks is a retired Aerospace Executive she is currently a Sickle Cell Disease Ambassador serving in multiple leadership roles at several entities in Southern California. She lives with immense gratefulness, appreciation, and thanksgiving enjoying her family, most especially her seven grandchildren. As a lifelong learner, Sheila loves reading, traveling, cooking, and snorkeling to name a few.

My black body is **Inquisitive.**

Jennifer Maritza McCauley is a writer, poet, and university professor. She is the author of WHEN TRYING TO RETURN HOME, a collection of short stories, and SCAR ON/SCAR OFF, a collection of poems. She is an assistant professor at the University of Houston-Clear Lake.

My black body is **Glorious.**

Fallen Matthews (She/Her) is an Afro-L'nu demigirl graduate candidate from Dalhousie University's interdisciplinary doctorate program. Although her project is anchored by psychoanalytic film theory in Cinema and Media Studies, other disciplines which span her research interests include Africana Studies, Artificial Intelligence, Indigenous Studies, and Gender Studies.

My black body is **Lost.**

Originally from Chicago, **Richard May** is a Professor of Writing at the Art Center College of Design in Pasadena and for the art department at California State University, San Bernardino. He also teaches in the African American Studies Department at California State University, Fullerton where his creative voice developed when he studied drawing and painting there as a student. As a scholar of the AFRICOBRA Art Movement, May's passion is teaching about African American art history.

My black body is **Sacred.**

JoAnne McFarland is an artist, poet, curator, and the Artistic Director of Artpoetica Project Space in Brooklyn which exhibits experimental works at the intersection of language and visual representation. McFarland has artwork in the permanent collections of The Library of Congress, The Columbus Museum of Art, and The Department of State, among many others. Her latest multimedia collection is Pullman published by Grid Books.

My black body is **Inviolable.**

xavia-margrith miles is a diarist, assemblist, and enchantress. xavia-margrith wields humorist sensibilities to cultivate intimacy with change, loss, desire, and divinity. Horror films, toys, and organic matter animate play and her exploration of wildness and interdependence. She is seeded in Minnesota's tundra, seasoned by Southern love, and Philly-fed.

My black body is **Wonder-full.**

Devin L. Mitchell is a graduate student at California State University, San Bernardino. He has been writing poetry since he was 14 years old to cope with difficult situations happening in life. He is inspired by writers and artists, such as Langston Hughes, S.E. Hinton, 2Pac, and Prince.

My black body is **Gold.**

Marcus Muscato is a graphical curator and online content creator who lives in Southern California. Marcus is a futurist, along with being an avid movie & gaming enthusiast.

My black body is **Astral.**

NOMAD the Poet is an award-winning LA Native poet, filmmaker, and activist who combines her passion for creative expression with her passion for healing and empowering her communities. She produces experimental films that combine prose, visuals, storylines, and character arcs to create an impactful, entertaining, and empowering cinematic experience; her latest award-winning short film, *The Sable Dragonfly: An Ode to My Black Female Body* delves into the complexities and beauty of navigating space as a black woman and can be found free online. NOMAD is set to have her first full-length collection of poetry, *Forged in Fire, Held in Love* published in June 2020.

My black body is **Cosmic**

Dr. Michael Andrew Owens a creative writer who emerges from a crucible of challenging life experiences that began in Chester, Pennsylvania in the 1950s, and continues to unfold after a recent transition to Southern California from Detroit, Michigan. Academically, he has received degrees in Political Science and Theology and has figured prominently in ecclesiastical and community leadership. He has a passion for the arts and gives expression to the stirrings in his spirit through sermonic proclamation, songwriting, and poetry.

My black body is **Indelible.**

Harry Palacio is the nephew of the Dominican Republic President Leonel Fernández and the Dominican consulate. Harry has read 3,214 books in his lifetime. Top 26 readers in the USA and top 49 readers globally as of 2022.

My black body is **Ennui.**

Pamela Peté affectionately called "Pamela D" has touched the hearts of many with her poetry. Her poetry has been called "Narrative Medicine" and has been included in the anthology *Storms of the Inland Sea* and published in several magazines and journals. Pamela holds an MFA in Creative Writing from UCR and is a USAF Veteran. However, being Nana to 21 grand and great-grandchildren is her greatest joy.

My black body is **Valuable.**

Karin Pleasant is a psychotherapist, dancer, drummer, podcaster, blogger, and recreational aerialist. She graduated in 2001 from the California Institute of the Arts with an MFA in writing and continues writing in her spare time whenever possible.

My black body is **Bountiful.**

Thomasina Sanders is a graduate of CSUSB with a degree in English literature. My mother, JoAnn Cooper was a writer, poet, and my first teacher and greatest inspiration. I have been performing spoken word throughout Southern California for over a decade.

My black body is **Complicated.**

Ahliah Sharp was born and raised in San Bernardino County to Joe and De Sharp. She has one brother: Joe Jr. and a 23-year-old son Jonah Cook. She is currently finishing her Ph.D. in industrial organizational psychology and has been an orator since she was a young child.

My black body is **Enough.**

S. Pearl Sharp. Spirit in this Black body for eighty/ played her part as "the 1st Negro" / met her Diaspora / polished the gift / word doula / motion storyteller / will sing you a poem / mandala: I see www.spearlsharp.com

My black body is **Precious.**

Calvin Shaw is from Jefferson City, Missouri, and currently resides in Colorado. He has works published in Lincoln Universities (MO) publication *Arts & Letters*, Volumes 23, 24, and 25. He has poems published in *Wingless Dreamer Publisher's Midsummer's Eve* & *My Unheard September* anthologies. When he is not watching sports or listening to music he is writing.

My black body is **Harmonious.**

Camryn G. Stevens is a soon-to-be CSUSB transfer student majoring in Anthropology and Theater Arts with an emphasis on Musical Theater. Her interests and talents include singing, writing, coaching basketball, cooking, and roller skating. She is so thankful for every opportunity God has brought her to pursue her passions.

My black body is **Mine.**

Linda Trice, Ph.D. a former resident of Sarasota, Florida taught Black History at the college level for many years. She has degrees from Howard University, The Center for Minority Studies, Columbia University, and Brooklyn Law School.

My black body is **Brilliant.**

Mitchell Washington enjoys spending time outdoors. He is an autodidact at heart and appreciates a good adventure.

My black body is **Mirrored.**

Deborah Tarver Waters is a retired elementary school teacher who now studies and teaches the Word of God, and preaches a little something, something too! Author of the book *Loving God*.

My black body is **Extraordinary.**

Dana Tenille Weekes explores the interiority of what human beings dare to do and are afraid to say. Her poems have been published in *A Gathering of the Tribes, Torch Literary, RHINO Poetry*, and in a forthcoming issue of *Obsidian*. She is the daughter of Bajan immigrants and is the first in her family to be born in the United States.

My black body is **Boundless.**

Sharon M. Williams is an author, educator, and business owner. Her most recent book is *Dark Days Light*. She also facilitates *Write with Ease*—a collage and writing workshop which emphasizes creativity, relaxation, and healing. Sharon can be reached anytime at shareeducation@att.net.

My black body is **Resilient.**

André Le Mont Wilson is a Black queer writer who won the 2022 Newfound Prose Prize for his chapbook, *Hauntings*. His work has appeared in *Obsidian: Literature & Arts in the African Diaspora, Umoja: ToPoJo Excursions: Black Diaspora Edition*, and *Rattle*. He teaches storytelling to adults with disabilities in Oakland.

My black body is **Gorgeous.**

Xclusively Taylor is a 16-year-old San Bernardino-based artist who works mainly in digital art. The principle theme in Taylor's work is African American Females. Her body of work demonstrates the beauty and diversity of black women.

My black body is **Unique.**

EDITOR

Romaine Washington, (she/her) is the author of two poetry collections, *Purgatory Has an Address* and *Sirens in Her Belly*. She is a two-time Pushcart Prize nominee and her writing has appeared in numerous publications. Notably, she has also been a part of a National Poetry Slam Team and has presented her work on local and national platforms such as KPFK, SoCal LA, and NPR.

As a graduate fellow of The Watering Hole in South Carolina and the Inland Area Writing Project at UCRiverside, Washington has been blessed with the opportunity to refine her creative writing skills alongside esteemed mentors and fellow writers. She actively contributes to Inlandia Literary Journeys and passionately facilitates writing workshops, providing aspiring writers with guidance and support. As an educator for over two decades, Washington has dedicated her time to nurturing and inspiring others in the literary community.

You can find out more about her and upcoming events on her website: www.romainewashington.com

Adinkra Symbols

Adinkra are symbols from Ghana that represent concepts or aphorisms.

HOPE
These black bodies are hopeful.

BEAUTY
These black bodies are bodacious.

FREEDOM
These black bodies are mystical.

JUSTICE
These black bodies are bearing witness.

PEACEMAKING
These black bodies are mindful.

LIFE'S DYNAMICS
These black bodies are eclectic.

KNOWLEDGE
These black bodies are enlightened.

TRANSFORMATION
These black bodies are transforming.

About Blacklandia

Inlandia Institute stands with our region's Black community in opposing racism and white supremacy and condemning police brutality and violence against Black people and communities everywhere. We stand with Black readers, writers, and poets. With Black families and youth. With Black educators and creators. With all who stand against injustice.

Inlandia Institute's Blacklandia Events Series was initiated in 2020 in response to the murder of George Floyd at the hands of the police on May 25th of that year. As an organization centered around the power of words, one that values speaking up and speaking out, Inlandia made a renewed and public commitment to providing a space for people in the Black community to come together, and from that arose a Black-led Black voices steering committee, and a new series of events, Blacklandia.

The Inaugural 2023 Blacklandia Anthology *These Black Bodies Are . . .* **is** dedicated to the memory of Ahmaud Arbery (May 8, 1994 - Feb. 23, 2020) and all those who have experienced racially-motivated violence, to the celebration of Opal Lee (October 7, 1926) the grandmother of Juneteenth and all who sojourn in solidarity for better.

About Inlandia Institute

Inlandia Institute is a regional literary non-profit and publishing house. We seek to bring focus to the richness of the literary enterprise that has existed in this region for ages. The mission of the Inlandia Institute is to recognize, support, and expand literary activity in all of its forms in Inland Southern California by publishing books and sponsoring programs that deepen people's awareness, understanding, and appreciation of this unique, complex and creatively vibrant region.

The Institute publishes books, presents free public literary and cultural programming, provides in-school and after school enrichment programs for children and youth, holds free creative writing workshops for teens and adults, and boot camp intensives. In addition, every two years, the Inlandia Institute appoints a distinguished jury panel from outside of the region to name an Inlandia Literary Laureate who serves as an ambassador for the Inlandia Institute, promoting literature, creative literacy, and community. Laureates to date include Susan Straight (2010-2012), Gayle Brandeis (2012-2014), Juan Delgado (2014-2016), Nikia Chaney (2016-2018), and Rachelle Cruz (2018-2020).

To learn more about the Inlandia Institute, please visit our website at www.InlandiaInstitute.org.

Inlandia Books

Pretend Plumber by Stephanie Barbé Hammer

Ladybug by Nikia Chaney

Vital: The Future of Healthcare, edited by RM Ambrose

Güero-Güero: The White Mexican and Other Published and Unpublished Stories by Dr. Eliud Martínez

A Short Guide to Finding Your First Home in the United States: An Inlandia anthology on the immigrant experience

Care: Stories by Christopher Records

San Bernardino, Singing an anthology edited by Nikia Chaney

Facing Fire: Art, Wildfire, and the End of Nature in the New West by Douglas McCulloh

Writing from Inlandia, an annual anthology (2011-)

In the Sunshine of Neglect: Defining Photographs and Radical Experiments in Inland Southern California,1950 to the Present by Douglas McCulloh

Henry L. A. Jekel: Architect of Eastern Skyscrapers and the California Style by Dr. Vincent Moses and Catherine Whitmore

Orangelandia: The Literature of Inland Citrus by Gayle Brandeis

While We're Here We Should Sing by The Why Nots

Go to the Living by Micah Chatterton

No Easy Way: Integrating Riverside Schools - A Victory for Community by Arthur L. Littleworth